The Future Necklace

The Future Necklace

Jessie Paddock

Scholastic Inc.

Copyright © 2022 by Jessie Paddock

All rights reserved. Published by Scholastic Inc., *Publishers since 1920*. SCHOLASTIC and associated logos are trademarks and/or registered trademarks of Scholastic Inc.

The publisher does not have any control over and does not assume any responsibility for author or third-party websites or their content.

This book is a work of fiction. Names, characters, places, and incidents are either the product of the author's imagination or are used fictitiously, and any resemblance to actual persons, living or dead, business establishments, events, or locales is entirely coincidental.

ISBN 978-1-338-72483-7

10 9 8 7 6 5 4 3 2 1   22 23 24 25 26

Printed in the U.S.A. 40

First printing 2022

Book design by Yaffa Jaskoll

For Momma

Chapter One

"The Dolphins are a strong team," Coach Puma said, her voice echoing off the tile walls of the indoor pool. Except for Coach Puma and the faint hum of the water filters, the space was otherwise silent. "But so are we. Let's start our Stingray season off strong."

Ellie Greene nodded solemnly. She sat in the center of the front row of the squeaky metal bleachers. Behind her, Ellie heard her teammates shift. They'd had a long week of practices. If Coach Puma said they were ready, they were ready, right?

Ellie wasn't so sure.

The spot just below the dip in her collarbone burned like an ember, just like it always did when she was worried. Ellie shivered beneath her damp bathing suit and tapped her cool fingertips, still pruned from an hour and a half of swim practice, against her blushing skin.

"Everyone knows what events they're swimming tomorrow, so no surprises," Coach Puma continued, marking off something with a pen on her clipboard.

Ellie nodded again. She'd be competing in the fifty-yard fly, fifty-yard free, and a leg of the freestyle relay. She had her sights set on a position in the individual medley—or IM—relay, where each athlete swam a different stroke, rotating through butterfly, backstroke, breaststroke, and finally freestyle. But her times hadn't made the cut. Not yet. During that first week of practices, Ellie was still a good 3.21 to 4.34 seconds behind the personal records she'd set the season before. She'd hoped her massive growth spurt over the summer (four inches in three months!) might give her a leg up but so far, not so much. These days Ellie sometimes felt like a stranger inside her own gangly body.

Ellie Greene was a water girl. Always had been, probably always would be. She felt more at home in the water than on land. Pool, ocean, pond, bathtub— it didn't matter. When she'd started swim team in third grade, something just clicked: the way her body felt smooth and weightless, her limbs and her lungs working together, soon each stroke was so practiced her brain could turn off once she launched into a freestyle or a lazy breaststroke. When she was in the water, the world was quiet. She could forget all her planning and training and just let her body take over.

Except that wasn't exactly what had been happening. Not lately. Not since the beginning of the seventh-grade season. Even in the pool, Ellie's brain felt busier than ever with "what-ifs," worrying and wondering about anything and everything. Though it didn't feel like she was swimming any slower, her times indicated otherwise, particularly in her favorite race, the fifty-yard fly.

"Transitions," Coach Puma said, then paused. Maybe for effect? Her shoulder blade–length braids were gathered in a low brown ponytail, and signature aviator sunglasses were propped on her forehead. In one year and counting, Ellie had never seen Coach Puma without sunglasses on her person, no matter the time of day. "Transitions are key."

Ellie pursed her lips. All week, they'd been practicing turns—or, as Coach Puma called them, *transitions*. Ellie was not a fan. The word echoed in her head constantly.

Transitions.

Each stroke required a different kind of turn—ahem, *transition*—between laps. For freestyle there was the flip turn; for butterfly there was the two-hand touch. Relays were a beast of their own, as the next swimmer could only dive off the starting block once their teammate swimming before touched the wall. Just like in an individual event, if a relay swimmer began before the starting beep, their team would be disqualified. (Disqualified or DQ: One of the scariest terms in all of swim and swim-adjacent vocabulary.) Coach Puma had the Stingrays practice transitions of all kinds over and over that first week of practice. Transitions, as it turned out, were complicated. But for Ellie, it wasn't just the in-pool transitions that proved challenging. It was also everything else.

Ellie hoped seventh grade would be different. Last year, as a pre-growth-spurted rookie, she'd faded into the shadows, often deferring to what her older, louder teammates said (and, boy, were they loud). Now that she was a seventh grader, and one of the taller Stingrays at that, Ellie had thought she'd feel more at home among the group.

So far, her expectation had not proved accurate.

Ellie preferred the actual swimming part of swim

team, not the transitions in between. Swimming, one stroke after the next, felt natural and predictable. But transitions, even those out of the pool, were proving wonky. All of them. Water-break transitions, between-drill transitions, gathering-belongings-in-the-locker-room transitions . . . there were probably more. And perhaps as a result, though Ellie couldn't totally understand the connection, her in-pool transitions were now jumbled as well. Coach Puma had called her out for stuttering the two-hand touch between butterfly laps (which, in competition, would be an immediate DQ) and Ellie'd gotten a nose full of water during her flip turns more than once (which was a real amateur mistake).

"Make sense?" Coach Puma asked, not so rhetorically. Behind her, Ellie's teammates murmured in approval. Ellie followed suit, though she truly had no idea what she was agreeing to. She'd gotten lost in her thoughts. Again. That had been happening a lot more lately.

Coach Puma continued. Ellie sat up a little straighter and fiddled with the elastic goggle strap that hung around her neck like a clunky hot-pink necklace. "As some of you may have noticed, and mentioned, our meet against the Druid Hills Riptides is early this season. Third meet of the year."

Some of Ellie's teammates chattered behind her. Ellie wondered what they were saying, though she had her guesses. The Riptides were their rivals, and last season, they'd lost to them in spectacular fashion. And by spectacular, that meant by two hundredths of a second. *Spectacular* was often synonymous with *devastating* when it came to swimming. For Ellie, the meet was particularly sour because she'd gotten disqualified due to a false start, something that had never, ever happened to her during competition before. It was humiliating, a terrible way to end the season, but awful mostly because she let her team-mates down. Due to her DQ, the pressure was on to win the last race of the meet. Snacks, their current co-captain and overall star, had gotten off to a good start, but in the end she didn't pull it off due to an incredible comeback from a swimmer in lane four. Nobody, including Ellie, had seen the Riptide come-back coming. Riptides were like that. They snuck right up on you.

Ellie shivered, goose bumps speckling her shins, thighs, and even kneecaps, though that spot below the center of her collarbone remained fiery as ever. Yes, she'd gotten taller, her feet had expanded two whole shoe sizes, but Ellie still worried as much as always.

"We don't need to think about the Riptide meet now," Coach Puma instructed, raising her voice over the heightened chatter. "Let's focus on what's right in front of us, the present task at hand. Any questions before I hand it over to the captains?"

Ellie's mind reeled. Truly, she wasn't quite sure where to start. Questions were pretty much all she had: *Do you think they'll start on time? Is the temperature of the Dolphins' home pool comparable to ours? Did anyone on the Dolphins have a growth spurt like mine over the summer? Will we be swimming in odd or even lanes?* There were probably more. Not to mention essentials, like *Will we win? Will I get off the block fast enough to get an early lead? Will I break my personal records? Will anyone be at the end of my (hopefully even) lane, cheering me on at the transition?* Questions upon questions that, unless Coach Puma had a way to see the future, would be impossible to answer.

Ahhh, a way to see the future. *Wouldn't that be nice*, Ellie thought wistfully.

"Yes, Joelle?" Coach Puma called, piercing Ellie's rumination with her sharp voice.

"So, I'm not sure if this is totally obvious or not," Joelle began, her hands fidgeting with the swim cap in her lap as she spoke. "But is the Dolphins' pool indoors? It's no big deal or anything, I just like to know ahead of time because of acoustics and sunscreen and stuff . . ." Joelle's voice trailed off and her eyes landed on the ground.

Joelle Pike was new. She'd just moved to their Phoenix suburb from the outskirts of Chicago, Ellie had overheard. She was a super-fast breaststroker, but that's all Ellie really knew about her teammate. Well, that and she had purple braces and had definitely not experienced an almost-supernatural growth spurt. Ellie recrossed her legs, positioning her limbs so they felt even just an inch shorter.

"Very much indoor," Snacks answered, calling from the opposite end of the bleachers as she unwrapped a package of peanut butter crackers.

Ellie's stomach grumbled. She was always starving at the end of practice. That morning, before school, Ellie's mom had mentioned they'd be having a special dinner. Probably as a gear-up for the first meet. Ellie's mom knew that Ellie'd been nervous about it all week. Hopefully, hamburgers from Everybody's were on the menu. Or sushi from RuSan's. Or pizza or subs or all the above.

"All right, on that note, captains, take it away," Coach Puma instructed, stepping aside for Sophie Choi (aka "Snacks") and Quinn James (aka "Top Five") to take center stage on the pool deck before their teammates.

Ellie had yet to receive a nickname. She was unclear if there was an official nicknaming ceremony, but a handful of the eighth graders exclusively answered to names that certainly were not on their birth certificates. Ellie wondered what hers might be . . . hopefully it would be funny. Maybe, if it stuck, she'd ride it out through college.

Snacks and Top Five stood before their team. Snacks had a lollipop tucked into the strap of her bathing suit. For quick access, presumably. Top Five had a number five shaved into the side of his head, his medium-brown skin contrasting against his dark brown hair. No doubt about it, he was top five in a lot of categories, not just his regional swim ranking. Top five tallest, top five loudest voices in all Arizona, top five in his knowledge of obscure pie flavors. According to him. Ellie dared to suggest that he might also be top five in most confident.

"Here we go," Snacks began.

"Here. We. Go," Top Five repeated.

"First meet of the season," Snacks added. "Go big, go bad, go—"

"Yellow!" Snacks and Top Five exclaimed in unison.

They sure were the dynamic duo. Had Snacks and Top Five rehearsed this? What must it feel like to have someone else finish your sentences? Ellie had that with her mom, but that wasn't the same. Maura Greene was cool and all, but she was still Ellie's mom. Different.

"Swim fashion is a thing," Top Five explained. "When you look good, you feel good, and when you feel good, you swim . . ."

"Better!"

"Kapow!"

Snacks and Top Five did a quick but complicated handshake that involved snapping and a subtle jazz hand.

"Tomorrow we wear all yellow. Key word *all*."

"Other key word, *yellow*," Top Five noted.

Before the captains could get another word in, Joelle raised her hand.

"Rookie on the left," Top Five said, pointing both hands in Joelle's direction.

"Yellow, like head to toe?" Joelle sure did have a lot of questions.

Ellie could relate. She'd been tempted to make the same inquiry herself. Also, what Ellie dared not ask was, if Stingray colors were purple and yellow, wouldn't all purple be easier? It was definitely more of a closet staple, Ellie figured, racking her brain for what yellow items even existed inside her home at large.

"Correct," Snacks confirmed. "Mono—"

"Chrome," Top Five concluded.

"Oh. Okay," Joelle said. Ellie watched Joelle pull out a metallic-silver Sharpie from her red swim bag and write something on the back of her hand.

"Stingrays always wear a team L-E-W-K on meet days. We're starting simple, but you can expect things to get—"

"Jazzier," Top Five said, a definite twinkle in his eye.

Ellie really had no idea what they meant by "jazzy." Sequins? Bow tie and top hat? It would be nice to know in advance in case she needed to make a stop at the thrift store. Her wardrobe ranged from simple to plain.

"Unless," Snacks said in a stage whisper that Coach Puma could definitely hear, "Coach P drops those fire warm-up jackets."

Ellie knew what Snacks was talking about. She sensed her teammates' ears perk up as well. Top Five made a not-so-subtle "Ahem." They were supposed to get warm-up jackets last season but "budget cuts are real," so they fell through the cracks. Team jackets were high on everybody's list of hopes for this season.

"Also, for those of you who care," Snacks said.

"Which really should be everyone," Top Five muttered under his breath.

"At the stroke of midnight, Mercury goes into retrograde for a whopping two weeks. Don't sign any contracts if you can help it," Snacks advised.

"Okay, great, thank you, Snacks and Top Five," Coach Puma said, stepping back in. Coach Puma was mega serious—she'd swum Division I in college, so maybe that had something to do with it—but always used her swimmers' nicknames. Ellie appreciated that. "Everyone be at the bus tomorrow by three fifteen sharp. Who can collect?"

Kickboard, flipper, buoy, swim paddle: Swimmers had lots of props used in practice that got strewn about the pool over the course of a training session.

Joelle shot her hand high in the air.

"Thanks, Joelle. You're on kickboards and flippers." Coach Puma scanned the bleachers before Snacks and Top Five volunteered to gather the rest. "See everyone tomorrow."

Practice was over. Ellie stretched her arms overhead, hanging back for a moment as her teammates filed off the bleachers and toward the locker room. Mike Perez (aka Hamburger Mike) described, for the billionth time, why mayo on a burger was an essential condiment. The seventh-grade "tornado"— a clique of four girls who Ellie had been in school with since kindergarten but also basically didn't know at all—chatted excitedly amongst themselves as they glided across the tiled pool deck. Eighth-grade power couple Tye Penn and Brianna Wheatley (in tandem referred to as "Tyanna") sauntered hand in hand, which reminded Ellie of her mom and her mom's boyfriend, making Tyanna seem impossibly mature. Joelle, hot on Snacks's and Top Five's tails, flipper in each hand, seemed to be asking more questions.

Ellie stood to go as Coach Puma approached.

"Hey, El, got a minute?"

Ellie nodded, speechless that Coach had used a pseudo-nickname when addressing her. It wasn't swim-team-goofy or anything, but still. The gesture, intentional or not, felt worth noting. Ellie perked up, shoulders (which were so sore!) back, and spine a little straighter.

"Of course, Coach," Ellie answered, then quickly added, "Puma," in case her coach was not into the name-shortening vibe.

"Okay, so I need to do some last-minute adjustments before submitting info for the lineup, and I have you on the fifty free, fifty fly, and free relay," Coach Puma said, eyes scanning over papers attached to a clipboard.

"Yep!" Ellie chirped. Those were the races she'd been focused on the last few days, the events she'd primarily swum last year, and the events she planned on for tomorrow.

"I'm going to drop you into the fifty back as well," Coach Puma explained as easily as if she were saying "The sky is blue" or "I had pancakes for breakfast."

"Backstroke?" Ellie confirmed, shocked. She hadn't competed in a backstroke race since elementary school. She never quite managed to get through an entire length of the pool without smashing into a lane line. Also, swimmer's neck, which really was a thing.

"Yeah, are you okay with jumping in? Brianna's shoulder is bothering her, so it would be great if you could step it up."

What could Ellie say? That she was terrified to swim a race that she hadn't practiced? She didn't want to let the team down by totally bombing? That surprises like this were very hard to prepare for on such short notice?

No. She couldn't say any of that.

"So, what do you think?" Coach Puma pressed.

Oops. Had Ellie zoned out again? Her brain felt like a shaken-up soda with a closed top, with nowhere for the carbonation to go.

So, Ellie replied, "Sure thing!"

"Great," Coach Puma said, jotting a note on her clipboard. Ellie was about to go, considering herself dismissed, when her coach asked, "You've seemed a bit distracted this season, Ellie. Anything on your mind?"

Is there anything that isn't on my mind? Ellie thought. *Will I ever get my times down? Will these extra four inches help my speed or just get in the way? Who will I talk to during water breaks? How often will we do drills where we have to partner up? Will I be able to pull off a win in my individual races? Can I make it through the opening meet without a DQ? If I do get a DQ, is my swimming career over?*

But Ellie didn't say any of that. She feared if Coach Puma knew any of her concerns, even if she did manage to drop enough time, no way would she put her on the IM relay squad.

"Nope! I've just been focusing on my visualizations more, so maybe that's part of it?" Ellie said, which was true, but also sort of not that true at the same time.

"Okay, well, try to stay in the present. Swimming

happens in the moment, not before or after. Remember that."

"Totally," Ellie acknowledged, though she was already thinking about what she'd be having for dinner and if she'd convince her mom to watch a movie after.

Chapter two

The moment Ellie walked into the apartment that she shared with her mom, she sensed that something was off. Not in a bad way, necessarily. But something was definitely *up*.

When Ellie's mom mentioned that they were having a special dinner, Ellie just assumed that meant medium-fancy takeout instead of box macaroni and cheese. Ellie's mom, though fabulous in basically every way, was no chef. It was a very like-mother, like-daughter kind of situation. Takeout, peanut butter and jelly, pasta with butter, cereal, and more takeout were the standard fare in the Greene household. Sometimes English muffin pizzas if they were feeling wild.

Ellie closed the door behind her, kicked off her rubber slides, and considered the space.

Music. Jazz, was it? There was definitely some

pitty-patty piano going on. That was unusual. Ellie and her mom were music-with-lyrics kinds of gals.

Ellie stepped down the hall, slowing as she passed the entrance to the dining room she'd probably only set foot in once. The lighting. Candles. In holders. And place mats—the rose-pink ones with the scalloped edges that made Ellie very nervous to eat on lest she spill. Which, let's be honest, she probably would.

Ellie inched closer to the kitchen. That's when she experienced the smell. No—*aroma* was more like it. It wasn't pizza. Pizza adjacent? There was definitely a red sauce involved. But it wasn't Amore's or LaFeni's or any of the usual Italian spots they ordered from. She was certain of that.

Ellie was no detective, but something was going on. The question was . . . what?

"Mom?" she called.

"We're in the kitchen, love!" Ellie's mom replied over the piano music. Now that Ellie thought about it, she didn't totally like this music, though she imagined some might consider it to be calming.

Ellie looked back over her shoulder at the dining table. There were three settings.

The kitchen vibe was a little more normal, at least. Ellie's mom leaned against the counter behind the kitchen island next to the oven, still in her lucky turquoise GO ON AND BUY THIS MANSION ABOVE ASKING PRICE, WHY DON'T YA? dress. She was a newly licensed real estate agent, which basically meant that she got dressed up every day, worked a lot of random times to show clients fancy properties, and also loved her job. Ellie was into it as much as she could be given that her mom might have to miss a few of her meets that season to host open houses for prospective buyers.

"What's going on?" Ellie asked suspiciously, noticing a huge, multicolored salad on the counter. Ellie and her mom knew that vegetables were important, obviously, but they were sort of on a twice-a-week intake schedule. They'd had a nearly unbearable amount of broccoli with their General Tso's chicken the night before; they weren't due for anything plant-based again until the weekend, at the earliest.

A voice came from behind the kitchen island. "Dinner will be ready in T minus ten."

Ellie's mom's boyfriend, Andy, appeared, fully decked out in a crimson apron that sort of accentuated the fact that he had dirty-blond hair but a red beard. Ellie had never seen the apron before. He held a bubbling tray of lasagna in his oven-gloved hands. The overhead light made his receding hairline glisten.

"Oh, hey," Ellie murmured. She hadn't realized that Andy was joining. Or cooking an elegant meal, apparently. Though with the three place mats, she probably should have, come to think of it.

Ellie had to admit, the lasagna smelled very good. Like, extremely, extremely good. So did what she really hoped was garlic bread inside a wrapping of aluminum foil next to the salad bowl.

"Go put your stuff up and change," Ellie's mom said with a smile. Her hair was down, exposing a few strands of silver among her absolute mane of maple syrup–brown tresses that Ellie had inherited. "Get out of your sweats real quick. We're pretending to be extra civilized tonight."

"Ball gown it is," Ellie joked. "Just gotta unpack my swim bag," she added, which, of course, her mom knew because that's what she always did right after practices.

"Can you turn the oven down to 325?" she heard Andy ask her mom as she walked out. Ellie chuckled.

She'd never seen her mom touch a button on that oven in her life.

Any swimmer who knew anything knew that mildew could be a real problem. Ellie was aware from experience. If she left a wet bathing suit or towel in her bag, forget about it. Most items in Ellie's life, including her hair and outer layer of skin, smelled at least faintly of chlorine (#poollife). She wasn't trying to add mildew to her already-aquatic olfactory disposition.

After each swim practice or meet, Ellie placed her swim bag—a purple backpack that was basically three times the size of a normal backpack—onto her desk chair and unpacked. She proceeded in the same order every time. It was something of a ritual. Just as every object in her bedroom had a place, every single item in Ellie's swim bag had a spot. Which meant that not only did she pack it the same way every time, but she did the same process in reverse whenever returning home from practice or a meet. Yes, Ellie had a capital-*P* Process.

Ellie opened all the zippers to air out the goggles, swim cap, and backup-goggles-backup-swim-cap pockets. She removed her toiletry kit—a neon-yellow pouch filled with shampoo, conditioner, lotion, and eardrops (part of her swimmer's ear prevention initiative)—and any wet bathing suit or towel. The only pocket she didn't touch was the small one on the top flap where she kept Sharpies and her lucky rubber-duck key chain with a mystery key to nowhere. Having a thoroughly packed and precisely organized swim bag was just one totally obvious and easy way to be and stay prepared.

Ellie's stomach growled. Coach Puma often reminded them that people used three times as much energy when in water compared to on land. After practices, Ellie's appetite was endless. Ellie diligently finished unpacking, threw on a pair of shorts and T-shirt that felt the most ball-gown adjacent, and returned to the kitchen for dinner.

The lasagna was delicious. Ellie hated to admit it, for no reason in particular, but it really was. Instead, she offered "Very hot" when Andy asked if it was cheesy enough for her. It was both hot and cheesy. Otherwise, Ellie focused on her food while her mom talked about a new house on the market with "a very impractical staircase but divine molding."

Ellie's mom and Andy gave each other a look as Ellie sat back down with a plate of seconds. They were always doing that: sharing these impossible silent exchanges that literally made no sense. Ugh, couples (eye roll).

"So, what's with all this nice stuff? Don't get mad at me if I spill. I haven't practiced my fancy manners in a while," Ellie said, taking another giant bite of saucy, noodly goodness, and probably not chewing with her mouth closed. As if on cue, she caught a drop of sauce in her hand right before it splashed onto the place mat.

Mom and Andy laughed a little more than her half joke really warranted. When Ellie and her mom had lived with her grandma for a bit after her parents got divorced, Mimi was always threatening to send both Ellie and her mom to "fancy manners school" if they didn't wash their dishes or chew with their mouths closed. It was unclear if such a place existed.

Mom sipped her water. If Ellie didn't know any better, she'd say her mom was nervous.

"Seriously, though, is this a setup? I know we have a good chance of beating the Dolphins tomorrow— Coach Puma said our lowest times are like at least three seconds better on free and fly, which puts us in a good place for those events and the relay," Ellie explained, repeating almost exactly what her coach had said at the end of practice a couple of hours earlier, though the flushed sensation in the center of her chest served as a reminder that her personal times had been unpredictable at best. "But don't you think it's a little early to celebrate?"

"Three seconds is a lot in swimming?" Andy asked.

Ellie resisted the urge to roll her eyes. Andy gave the distinct impression that athletics were not in his repertoire. "It's a lifetime."

"Ahhh, okay. In soccer, three seconds goes by pretty quick."

"Cool," Ellie replied. She eyed the salad bowl. So far, Andy had been the only one to help himself.

"I'm sure the meet tomorrow is going to be great," Mom began. "An undoubted success."

Ellie wasn't so sure how her mom knew that, but okay.

Ellie's mom put her fork down and weaved Andy's hand into hers. "But there's actually something else we wanted to talk to you about, love."

"Soooo . . . are we going on vacation again? If so,

please, please, please can we go snorkeling? I'll call ahead for reservations and everything!"

After school let out last June, Andy had taken them on a trip to Mexico. He and Mom hadn't been dating too long at that point, but who could argue with a beach vacation? Not Ellie. The highlight had been the snorkel portion of the week. Ellie's mom had gotten too seasick, and Andy, out of some sort of boy-friend obligation or something, insisted on staying on the boat with her. Ellie, however, had really made the most of the experience. She'd seen a barracuda and a real live stingray. Both were more aerodynamic (water-dynamic?) in person. If she ever got to go snor-keling again, she'd see if she could get her hands on a waterproof camera.

Ellie blinked away the memory of tropical waters and returned to the present, realizing Mom had been saying something.

". . . and with all of that in mind, we wanted to share that . . . we're getting married."

Ellie almost choked on a noodle.

"Wh-what?" she stammered.

"I love Maura—I mean, your mother—very much," Andy said, turning to Ellie's mom.

So do I, Ellie thought. Instead, she managed to squeak, "Congratulations."

"Andy proposed at the zoo," Ellie's mom gushed. The zoo? Wasn't that kind of juvenile? Since when did Mom go to the zoo? Then, quieter, to Andy, she added, "Best surprise ever."

Why were engagements always surprises? That sounded awful, as far as Ellie was concerned. Why would anyone want to be surprised with life-altering news? Much better to have it all planned out like rational humans.

"I'm really excited and honored to become part of your family," Andy said softly, still holding Mom's hand.

Andy could benefit from bigger glasses. From a fashion perspective. His were extremely outdated. They were probably the kind that turned into sunglasses automatically when he was outside. Oh, gosh, what if all three of them had to start going to the zoo together? Ellie wasn't a fan of seeing animals in captivity. She'd never told her mom that, but then again, she didn't think she had to. It hadn't come up. Would it now?

"El, talk to us," Ellie's mom said.

"Um, hi," Ellie said before taking a giant gulp of water. Suddenly she was so, so thirsty. Little-known fact: Even though it doesn't show up the same way, people sweat just as much when swimming as when exercising out of the water. Hydration was still super important. Ellie drained her glass.

"I know this is a lot to take in." Ellie's mom had dropped Andy's hand, and now gazed at her daughter.

Ellie stared at her plate and didn't blink. A fancy lasagna dinner where they were all sitting in the uncomfortable chairs totally still without anything else to do but talk or look down at the plate really felt like the absolute wrong way to have this conversation. If it was up to her mom, she would have broken the news while watching a show or eating takeout at the kitchen counter. This must have been Andy's influence. Obviously. The remains of the red sauce on her plate looked sort of like a palm tree. A palm tree on fire, burning right up. Everything around her felt very heavy, intense, loud, and quiet,. She needed some air.

"May I please be excused? I just remembered that I need to do my pre-meet visualization prep before I get too tired. I'm going to the pool, just to sort of get into race vibe, okay?" Ellie stood, not waiting for an answer. "Thanks for the lasagna, it tasted super homemade."

Ellie didn't look either at her mom or Andy before darting out the front door and down the stairs toward the closest body of water.

Chapter Three

Ellie sat with her legs dangling in the lukewarm water. The Inman Terrace Apartments pool was shaped like a large kidney bean. Not the best for lap swimming, but better than nothing. Ellie often found herself there, whether she was working on a technical aspect of her butterfly stroke, or if she was in need of a good float. Normally, it was also her choice place for pre-meet visualization, a practice she'd started after reading that a lot of athletes, specifically Olympians, credited visualization as a major part of their success. But that evening, as the remnants of the golden hour light faded into the blue hour, the final traces of the sun reflecting from the sky and down onto the earth delicately filtering all below with a blue tint, race-day visualization was the last thing on Ellie's mind.

The blue hour was a short and special time at the end of the day. For years, Ellie thought it was something her mom made up on their first girls' trip to the Florida Panhandle with Ellie's aunt Kristina. Turned out, it was actually a real thing. That was the trip where she got stung by a jellyfish, but that didn't really matter because it was also when she officially learned how to swim. Blue hour took place after the sun dipped below the horizon but before the world turned completely dark, the remaining rays bouncing off the sky, emitting a sapphire filter upon the world. Something about that blue light made life feel especially soft, calming Ellie like a perfect sweatshirt on a cool night. It was the first time in a while that Ellie had been to the pool at that time of day. The cocoon of stucco apartment buildings surrounding the shared space, harsh and chalky in the afternoon, appeared friendlier.

Ellie and her mom had lived in the Inman Terrace Apartments for years. This was their second unit in the complex; over the summer they upgraded from a two- to a three-bedroom. Ellie didn't really see why they needed an extra room—their old place was cozy and fine—but her mom had raved about something she referred to as "great southern exposure" and suggested they "shake it up!" She also had said, now that

Ellie was thinking about it, "You never know when you might want more space." Had she said that, or was Ellie remembering incorrectly?

Married, huh? Was that really necessary? It felt like such an extreme choice. And really out of nowhere. It wasn't like she'd been dating Andy all that long. And it wasn't something she'd ever talked about, even when they went to Aunt Kristina's wedding last year. Ellie truly had never seen that coming. It wasn't that Andy was so bad or anything; it just felt like things were fine the way they were. Her dad had moved to Denver for work two summers ago, so it had been just Ellie and her mom for a while now, though Dad made a point to visit every couple of months. Her mom had had different boyfriends over the years, but she'd never threatened to actually marry any of them.

"Stepdad," Ellie whispered into the receding blue light. "Stepfather?"

Both sounded strange coming out of her mouth. Not because she hadn't said those words before. No, she knew of plenty of people with stepparents. But the term had never been applied personally. Never belonged to her.

My stepdad, Andy, Ellie imagined saying as she introduced him to Coach Puma or a teammate or . . . someone. It didn't sound right. Not yet, at least. Would it ever? She'd never really known what to call the man. Her mom referred to him as Andrew, which was strange because he always introduced himself as Andy. Ellie couldn't recall if she'd ever addressed him by name. She'd have to figure something out.

Transitions.

Coach Puma's oddly all-encompassing word came to mind again. "Transition" seemed like too calm of a way to put it, though. Unlike her flip turn, the upcoming shift on the horizon felt inevitably clunky, awkward, and anything but smooth. Ripe for a disqualification of some sort.

Things were about to change. Ellie didn't know how, exactly, but she was certain of it. Would they still get to go on girls' trips with Aunt Kristina, or would Andy have to come? A table for three, not a table for two. And the big thing they hadn't talked about: They'd all live together at some point. Andy would probably move in, right? When? Could they put that off until after the wedding, or would that be weird? There were probably more changes in the future. More than she could even imagine. It was those ghostlike question marks—inevitable alterations that she couldn't yet anticipate—that unnerved Ellie the most. How could she prepare if she didn't know what was coming?

A lone verdin with its unmistakable yellow head flew by, highlighting the full moon that had already appeared in the sky so, so, so far away. The pressure of the pool water around her ankles and calves felt like a hug.

It felt like so much was changing around her, and if Ellie didn't figure out something quick, she'd be caught two strokes behind. If only she could see what was coming, then she could plan ahead accordingly and the answers would be clear, the transitions less clumsy.

Ellie sighed.

Behind her, Ellie heard familiar voices murmuring. She snuck a look over her shoulder to find Mom and Andy standing just outside the sliding glass door on the terrace. The lookout spot was another plus of the new apartment. Ellie's mom could easily supervise solo swim practices from up there. Sometimes they'd had entire conversations, Ellie's mom calling over the railing, Ellie treading water, an eavesdropping neighbor the furthest thing from their minds. But Andy's presence made the balcony appear cramped.

Ellie swished her feet, watching the ripples reverberate across the pool's surface. Blue hour had come and gone; evening officially descended. The moon caught her eye again. She remembered what Snacks had said at practice about Mercury. Well, actually, she didn't really remember what her teammate had said. She just knew she said something. Ellie let her gaze drop and was about to drag herself away from the pool when a flash from the bottom of the deep end caught her eye. No, not a flash. More of a twinkle—a sneaky wink or a coy wave.

An invitation.

What was the object catching the light from the moon overhead? A dog toy? Aluminum foil? Not-so-buried treasure? A literal barracuda?

Ellie tilted her head to get a better look. The mystery item once again caught the light of the enormous moon. Ellie couldn't refrain. Without another thought, she jumped into the pool, clothes on, to retrieve the enchantment on the bottom of the deep end.

Moments later, Ellie stood in the shallow end, waist deep in water. Her wet T-shirt clung to her shoulders, the tip of her sopping ponytail floated in the water, and in her hands she held the most mesmerizing necklace she'd ever seen.

At a glance, the delicate silver chain and key-shaped charm were ordinary, providing an ample stage for the small blue stone on top of the key. The stone looked like it was made of frozen pool water: clear, frosty blue, and dazzling, though not overly flashy. Ellie was entranced. Something about the item held her attention; she didn't want to look away. The necklace, simply put, seemed to quiet all the other noise in her brain, if not just for a moment. Ellie stood in the pool, holding the charm and chain as carefully as if it were a just-hatched barracuda. She felt like the newfound piece of jewelry was made purposefully for her.

Ellie closed her right fist around the charm and waded out of the pool. Despite the temperature, goose bumps dotted her ever-tanned olive skin. Hand clutching the necklace, Ellie closed her eyes and shivered.

Suddenly, under the tint of a subtle blue filter, an

image of a donut without a hole, covered in a layer of sparkling purple sugar crystals, appeared in her mind's eye. The picture was clear and steady. Real. A moment later, the image dissolved. Ellie snapped her eyes back open, half expecting to see the donut waiting for her at the edge of the pool. Of course, it wasn't.

Was that déjà vu? Ellie wondered. She'd never really understood what that term meant, not having experienced it before. Maybe she'd gotten her first taste? No. Déjà vu related to something that had already happened. Right? The bizarre image of the cupcake felt more like a premonition.

Bonkers.

Ellie clasped the necklace around her neck, then fell back into the pool and let herself float on her back. That's what she loved about being in the water; gravity wasn't so much a thing. Water held you and wouldn't let you fall.

Maybe she'd been too rude to her mom and Andy. He had made a very good lasagna. She couldn't blame him for wanting to marry her mother; Maura Greene was the literal best. If her mom loved him, well, then the whole getting-married thing couldn't be too bad. Right? Ellie wasn't so sure, but maybe.

Maybe.

Ellie thought and floated for a few more minutes, gazing at the quickly darkening sky. Next to the moon, Ellie spotted a single star. Otherwise, the sky was clear. Rarely did it rain in Arizona.

The apartment was quiet when Ellie returned. She tried to let herself air dry, but since it had been a while since she'd done a fully clothed dunk, she'd forgotten how drippy waterlogged clothes could get. She tiptoed down the hallway toward the kitchen to grab a glass of water. On her way past the dining room, she saw the candles had been blown out and the table cleared. Only a single stack of fancy rose place mats remained.

Ellie arrived in the kitchen and stopped in her water-soaked tracks. She couldn't believe her eyes. On the island, resting on top of a neatly torn paper towel, sat a donut without a hole, dusted in sparkling purple sugar crystals. There was also a note, written on a piece of pale yellow lined paper. The handwriting was precise and unfamiliar.

Dear Ellie,

Good luck in your meet tomorrow. I made a batch of these last night (still toying with the recipe—let me know what you think!). I hope you enjoy! Go, Stingrays!

Andy

Ellie put down the note and stared at the treat. She loved donuts. Loved, loved, loved. Ellie picked up the baked good and took a huge bite. The dough was sweet but not too sweet, light but not too airy, and . . . what was that in the middle?

Ellie pulled the donut away from her mouth and looked at the center. Jelly donuts were predictable, and she'd often enjoyed the custard inside a Boston cream. But this was different. New. Never before experienced in her donut-eating career. Ellie took another giant bite, enjoying the delicious (and probably homemade) taste of caramel. She hadn't expected that.

"Not bad, huh?" Ellie's mom said, appearing in the doorway. She'd changed out of her fancy clothes and into her favorite sky-blue sweats. A pink scrunchie held her hair in a high, floppy bun.

"Seriously," Ellie mumbled, her mouth full. She was definitely going to lick her fingers.

As if reading Ellie's mind, her mom said, "There's one more, but don't even think about eating it without me."

"Don't be so sure," Ellie teased.

"Good swim?" Mom asked, gesturing toward her wet hair. And wet clothes. And wet . . . Ellie noticed that she was, in fact, standing in a puddle.

"Oh, yeah. Sort of a spur-of-the-moment thing."

Ellie's mom laughed. "That's what it seemed like. Spur of the moment can be good. Why don't you go shower and I'll mop up behind you."

Ellie turned to go.

"And one more thing, love." Ellie's mom reached out and placed her open hand over Ellie's heart.

Ellie's shoulders relaxed. It felt as if some ice she hadn't realized was there was starting to thaw. Ellie stepped closer—despite her growth spurt, her wingspan was a little shorter than her mother's—and returned the gesture. Hands on hearts. It was their version of a secret handshake. Ellie sometimes did it to herself, but it didn't have the same effect.

"I know this is big," Mom began. "And it might feel

like a lot is going to change. And some things will. But not the important stuff, okay? Remember: Just a hole in the ground with water in it. Okay?"

Ellie paused. That was something her mom said to her before her very first swim meet five years ago. Ellie had been nervous—so scared, in fact, that right before her first event, she ran to her mom crying, begging to leave. It was hard for her to believe now, but the pool felt so big and terrifying, not because she couldn't swim, but something about competing made the familiar space seem so different in Ellie's young eyes. *It's just a hole in the ground with water in it*, Ellie's mom had said. Now, years later, it was their own inside joke, a reminder that something might seem overwhelming but not to jump to conclusions about the outcome.

"Okay," Ellie said, though she wondered how her mom could be so certain. The future, in basically every way possible, felt foggier than ever. Beneath the gentle pressure of the heel of her mom's hand on her sopping T-shirt, Ellie felt the charm around her neck press into the spot right below the dip in her collarbone. The key was cool against her warm skin.

Chapter Four

Ellie woke up early on meet days.

Well, she always woke up early, but when competition was on the horizon, she made a point not to hit snooze even once. Swimming had a lot to do with confidence, and confidence came, in part, from a consistent routine. Meet days always began with her visualizations.

After one half of a still-delicious caramel-filled donut (she needed to remember to thank Andy next time she saw him . . . ugh) and a protein shake with enough spinach to get her through the weekend, Ellie returned to her room. She set her timer to ten minutes, just so she didn't lose track, and settled onto her special cartoon-dolphin-blue visualization cushion. Time to begin.

Ellie took another deep breath; three counts in, pause at the top, three counts out. She repeated the pattern twice more. On her fourth inhale, Ellie closed her eyes and imagined her fifty-yard freestyle race unfolding in perfect fashion. She envisioned how it would look, feel, and sound:

Walking up to the starting block. Rubber mats under my feet. Don't look at the competition, don't look at the stands, focus, breathe. Step onto the block. Right foot forward, just at the edge . . .

Ellie continued, experiencing everything from the starting beep to the dive into the water, the steady pace of the first lap, the swift flip-turn transition, and the acceleration into the finish. She imagined what it would feel like to emerge, breathless, in first place.

Ellie repeated the exercise with her leg of the freestyle relay, adjusting the start to incorporate jumping off the block when the swimmer before her hit the wall as opposed to the starting beep.

That brought her to the fifty fly. Her favorite race, but also the one with which she'd had the most challenges recently. Her best time that season was 4.24 seconds behind her personal record. An eternity. Ellie began the visualization like the previous two, but only made it through most of the first lap before her mind started to wander, venturing from the ideal future to the hypothetical.

What if I mess up the two-hand touch and get disqualified? I could stutter my hands like all those times in practice this week. Then it would be like a billion times harder for the Stingrays to win! What if my teammates make fun of me? What if the Dolphins make fun of me? What if the spectators make fun of me? What if Coach Puma never lets me swim the race again?! Ellie caught her mental tangent and diligently began again.

Step on the starting block. Stare straight ahead. Breathe in. Eyes on the water, just below the backstroke flags. Ugh, backstroke! I can't believe I'm swimming that race too! I haven't swum backstroke in competition in years! Is my neck even strong enough to make it two laps?

Shoot. She'd gone off track again. Ellie shook out her shoulders, then tried a third time.

Dive the exact moment the starting beep sounds. Glide through the water. Three full strokes before a gulp of air. Keep the pace steady. Approach the wall. Two-hand touch is coming. No matter what, don't stutter. Two hands, two hands, TWO HANDS!

Ellie stopped. Again. That's not how her ideal race would go, obsessing about the turn as she approached the halfway point. Ideally, she'd be cool, calm, collected; prepared.

Ellie tried to revisualize again and again, starting from the moment her body glided into the pool, but it was no use. If her mind didn't go to an ill-fated DQ, she found herself obsessing over the outcome of the meet or wondering why Coach Puma had chosen her of all people to fill in at backstroke. She tried switching positions, uncrossing her legs, balancing her palms faceup on her knees in full meditation mode, and even leaning against the wall for support. Nothing worked. Demoralized, Ellie let her hand wander to her collar. She wove the delicate chain in her fingers and felt the cool surface of the charm against her thumb as she made one last effort to visualize a backstroke race.

Suddenly, an entirely different vision appeared in Ellie's mind. It didn't feel like a distraction, though, not quite, and it wasn't a scene she'd conjured intentionally. And again, that blue light.

Joelle: giant khaki pants and a tan T-shirt, the bland colors contrasting against a backdrop of purple lockers, crouching in front of a spill of books, notebooks, and—

The timer went off. Ellie snapped her eyes open, replacing the funny vision with the view of her bedroom wall. Just as abruptly as the flash appeared, it was gone. That sure was weird. She'd had that similar déjà-vu sensation except, again, she couldn't recall seeing Joelle clambering around on the ground like that. Ever.

Bonkers.

Well, not exactly the pre-meet focused session she'd hoped for. She'd just have to spend a little extra time during warm-ups once she got to the pool. Hopefully, her events wouldn't be up first so she could take some time to herself to mentally prepare while her teammates swam the opening races.

Sweating her brains out, Ellie arrived at Mariposa Middle in an extremely seasonally inappropriate outfit. The all-yellow thing . . . that was a challenge. She'd cobbled together an ensemble that could only be described as bizarre. The main yellow item she'd excavated from deep in the coat closet was a bright yellow raincoat, similar to the one that little kids wear, complete with a hood. Neon-yellow leggings from an old Halloween costume and a random yellow scrunchie from her mom's bathroom topped the look. In the way back of her mom's sock drawer she'd found no yellow socks, but a random gold scarf and a yellow beanie that had certainly received little use. She'd grabbed both, just in case. Just in case of what, she wasn't sure, but having extra of anything was right in line with general preparation protocol.

The raincoat—a garment she didn't have much experience with because it only rained summers in their Phoenix suburb (why did they even own that thing?)—could double as an oven. That rubber material sure didn't breathe. Ellie was tempted to take it off, but she spotted Snacks and Top Five as she approached the front steps leading to the school's entrance. Decked out in a sunshine tie-dye set and a vintage neon windbreaker-material ensemble, Ellie suspected they'd been saving these looks for this very moment. Ellie felt more ridiculous than ever in her mismatched puzzle of an outfit, though grateful her raincoat offered a solid pop of color. No way could she take it off now that she saw when they'd said monochrome, they really meant monochrome.

"That's how we rock it!" Snacks called Ellie's way.

"Kaboom!" Top Five added.

"Go, Stingrays!" Ellie chirped, doing her best to keep her chin up. Despite the compliment, Ellie still felt like the most discombobulated human in Mariposa swim team history.

And under the seal of her raincoat, she was also soon to be the most dehydrated. Ellie made a beeline for the closest fountain to fill her water bottle. Her liter thermos was just about at capacity when she heard a crash behind her. Though it was initially unclear what exactly caused the commotion, Ellie's jaw nearly dropped when she turned around.

"I knew it!" she cried.

To which Joelle, crouching on the floor over a pile of spilled books and notebooks, dressed head to toe in khaki, looked up and replied, "You did?"

Ellie panicked. She didn't really know why that had slipped out. She rushed over to help her teammate, whose blandly attired physique contrasted against the wall of purple lockers.

"Oh, gosh, thanks," Joelle said, sounding just as frazzled as Ellie felt. "I still can't figure out my way around these halls. I was going that way but then I realized I had to go the other way, and then the kid with the fanny pack purse was playing imaginary foot-ball or something with the dude who has that hair . . ." Joelle made a motion with her hands that implied snakes growing out of someone's skull.

"Ugh, Liam and Kenny," Ellie said, knowing exactly who she was talking about.

"Yeah, them," Joelle muttered. "Anyway, thanks." Then, finally, looking up at Ellie, she blurted, "Whoa, you did it!"

Now it was Ellie's turn to be confused. "Huh?"

"Your clothes. The yellows. It's just such a specific color," Joelle complained. "All I had was this sort of yellow . . ."

"Adjacent," Ellie said, finishing her sentence.

"Exactly. Yellow adjacent. I'm not sure that's going to cut it. You haven't seen Snacks or Top Five yet, have you?" Joelle looked panicked. At this rate, there was no way she'd make it through the day without spilling the entire contents of her backpack again.

"Hey, I got you, actually," Ellie assured. She unzipped her backpack to retrieve the scarf and beanie. "Not sure you can get away with the beanie on your head because of—"

"Mrs. Lao, yeah," Joelle said knowingly, referring to the vice principal.

"Maybe you can just hold it or something." Ellie handed her teammate the accessories.

"Thanks," Joelle said. "Really, such a lifesaver."

"Go, Stingrays," Ellie said for the second time that morning, but this time, she didn't need to work so hard to keep her voice steady.

"Go, Stingrays!" Joelle cheered, wrapping the scarf around her neck.

The high of the scarf-and-beanie handoff didn't last for long. The morning was a blur, Ellie hardly absorbing anything in her first few classes, even failing to correctly measure the angle of a trapezoid in geometry, her favorite subject. With each period, Ellie found herself increasingly jittery. The meet was all she could think about. Would they pull off a win? Would she swim fast enough? Would she manage a two-hand touch or panic? Who would she sit with on the bus? Would she sit with anyone on the bus? Would she get a cramp mid-meet? Would aliens descend mid-relay?

Okay, she wasn't really worried about the last one, though if she had some assurance an extraterrestrial invasion was out of the question, that would be fine too.

Unlike the morning, the afternoon dragged on and on. Ellie could have sworn the clock was moving backward, though her thoughts about the meet felt like an internal motor. By the last period of the day, social studies, she felt like her mind had swum a thousand laps. If she could swim as fast as the thoughts racing through her brain, she'd set a world record that afternoon, no doubt about it.

Finally, classes were done for the day. Ellie met her team by the near corner of the school's parking lot and put on her headphones. They were the oversized kind. Nobody except for Ellie knew they were broken.

Another pre-meet ritual: headphones with no music. It wasn't that she didn't find music motivational, but Ellie usually spent so much time deciding on which tune to pick, hypothesizing if it would have the desired emotional effect, considering if a song like "Dream Reality" would make her happy, sad, distracted, or hyper. Too risky to leave it up to chance. But putting on headphones was necessary.

Ellie settled into an open row near the front of the

bus and stared out the window. Behind her, her team-mates talked excitedly. Ellie heard some muffled snippets about swimming, though mostly they were talking about anything but. Tyanna seemed to be interviewing Top Five about various categories of his top-five-ness for the school newspaper. Part of her was curious about what the Tornado Girls found so funny or what Hamburger Mike meant when he said, "The leap came before the frog! I promise!" but she remained seated. Across the aisle, Joelle stared out the opposite window, small earbuds tucked into her ears. Maybe Joelle wasn't listening to any music either.

When the Stingrays arrived at the Dolphins' home facility, Ellie immediately went to check the heat sheet taped to the pool wall by the spectator bleachers.

Heat sheet: a grid with every competitor's name that served as a road map for the meet ahead, list-ing the order of events, heats (if necessary), lane assignment, and best times per event for each swim-mer. Though swimmers generally knew their events prior to a meet, the heat sheet provided all the perti-nent details. The swimmers with the fastest times were assigned middle lanes. For a dual meet like this one (just two schools competing), there was only one heat per event, but come the end-of-season invitational, there'd be two, sometimes more.

Ellie pulled a purple Sharpie from her swim bag. She liked to write down her event information on the inside of her forearm for easy reference. Just as she'd hoped, her first race, the fifty fly, was the third event. She'd be able to take some time for last-minute visualizations slash get-in-the-zone prep during the first two events. Her fifty free was fifth; second to last was the freestyle relay; and, finally, the dreaded backstroke race. Her schedule was booked.

Ellie joined her teammates in the locker room and quickly changed into her racing suit. She scraped her long milk-chocolate hair into a low bun and fitted her swim cap over it. Goggles in hand, she stepped to the mirror over the sink to see if there were any stray hairs she'd need to tuck in. Though she'd smooshed her head into a latex swim cap a gazillion times by now, she still liked to do the finishing touches with her reflection in view. The sink came up to Ellie's thighs. Last year when she'd been in this particular locker room, she remembered the porcelain hitting her hip bones.

Satisfied with her cap fitting, Ellie gazed in the mirror. She was tall all right, but her arms looked strong, felt strong. What did she have to worry about? Before Ellie could think to answer, she noticed her new chain glistening around her neck. The blue on the charm still managed to glow in the fluorescent light. Ellie never swam in jewelry; not that it was officially prohibited or anything, but more frowned upon. Jewelry and athletics in general did not mix. She moved to unclasp the chain but hesitated. It was just long enough that she could easily tuck the charm beneath the collar of her suit without creating any extra drag. Ellie couldn't say why, but her gut told her to keep the necklace on.

Ellie hustled to the deck to begin warm-ups. After the long anticipatory day, she was eager to get into the pool already. "It's just a hole in the ground with water in it," Ellie said to herself as she jumped in and began her first lap of the day.

Mariposa swim meets had a bad habit of starting somewhere between seven to eighteen minutes late. Ellie knew—she'd kept track last season. For the first time ever, though, Ellie didn't mind. She still wanted to get an extra visualization round in before she had to swim. The additional time would be useful.

Of course, that day, the meet started right on time (okay, a minute late, but still).

Ellie noticed her mom dart into the stands just as the swimmers for the first event were taking their places behind the starting blocks. No Andy. Would he attend all their meets once they got married? Would he start coming to more before they got married? When were they getting married, anyway? Ellie realized that part of the arrangement had never been discussed. She sort of wanted to know the answer, but she also sort of didn't.

"Event one. Boys' fifty-yard breaststroke," the announcer called from her seat under a makeshift tent.

Top Five, Hamburger Mike, and two seventh graders stepped onto the blocks. The non-competing Stingrays closed in on the length of the pool along lane eight to cheer. Snacks planted herself at the end of lane six so she could shout words of encouragement in Top Five's face when he flip-turned. Ellie, however, hung back by the bleachers. She got her broken headphones from her swim bag and found a spot to stand facing the wall, as far from the action as she could manage.

Explosive cheers indicated that the starting race was underway. Ellie heard Snacks's voice above the rest. She sure had pipes.

Ellie did her best to quickly run through her fifty-yard free, free relay, and fifty-yard fly but kept finding herself distracted. As the meet pressed on behind her, she felt the pressure mount. Truly, meditating among the racket of dozens of cheering people and intermittent announcements, all under the extremely high ceiling that only made the acoustics worse, wasn't exactly the ideal. But what else could Ellie do? She saw no other way to prepare.

Ellie had yet to begin her backstroke visualization when she heard an eruption of cheers and a whistle. Time to get on the pool deck for her first race. Ellie ditched the headphones and speed walked (no running on the pool deck, duh) to the water's edge.

Ellie's heart beat faster and faster as she approached the starting block behind lane three. She mimed a two-hand touch in the air before stepping onto the block. What if she stuttered at the turn, just as she'd been doing in practice all week? That would be an automatic disqualification. How disappointing, not to mention embarrassing, to get a DQ in the first meet of the season!

"Swimmers, take your marks!"

Ellie nudged her right toe to the tip of the block and leaned forward, her fingers grazing the bumpy edge. As she glanced up, she saw that nobody stood at the end of her lane.

Two hands. Two. Hands. Whatever you do, two hands, Ellie chanted in her mind. *No matter what, two—*
BEEP!

Ellie dove forward after a split second's hesitation. Water shot up her nose—her dive was too shallow. Already out of breath somehow, Ellie kicked her feet in a wavelike motion and broke through the surface.

Five yards down.

Then ten.

Then fifteen.

Ellie saw the wall as she came up for breath. It almost seemed like the wall was coming toward her rather than the other way around.

Twenty yards.

There it was. Was her stroke timed right? No. She needed to shorten it. But too late.

Whatever you do, two hands, two hands!

Was one of her hands already in front of the other? No, she wouldn't do that. But maybe it was? She couldn't be sure. But she had to be sure. The wall was right there. For a second, Ellie paused, slowing her momentum. Deliberately, so there was no doubt in her mind or anyone's mind, she smacked the wall with both hands.

Only then did she remember the race wasn't done. She had to actually turn. Frenzied, Ellie maneuvered her body in the other direction and pushed away from the wall. The splash from her competitor's kick in the next lane over smashed against her face. Ellie couldn't help but notice she was a full body length behind the swimmers on either side.

Time to turn on the jets.

Which Ellie did. She swam as fast and as hard as her arms and legs would allow. When she hit the wall at the end—two hands again—panting, heart racing, she saw that she'd come in an unimpressive seventh out of eighth. She didn't need to see her time to know that she'd broken no records.

On her way to towel off she passed by Coach Puma.

"Good job with the turn," she said.

Ellie couldn't help but wonder if Coach Puma was just being nice.

Come the final few events of the meet, the Stingrays and the Dolphins were neck and neck. Both of Ellie's freestyle races, the individual and relay, were . . . fine. Nothing catastrophic, but she'd broken no personal records. Truthfully, she'd spent the moments leading up to each race and half her time in the pool thinking about the backstroke race she still hadn't managed to properly visualize!

Ellie stood behind the Tornado Girls as the boys competing in the fifty backstroke arranged themselves behind the starting blocks. The Dolphins' pool was cavernous. All indoor pools had that vibe, but unlike the Mariposa complex, the Dolphins had a large spectator area on a second level, looking over the deck. Sort of like a coliseum. Green and white flags were draped over the width of the pool—one strand at each end about five yards from the end. Backstroke flags, they were called, so the swimmer could gauge how close they were from the wall when approaching. Ellie had a vague idea of how many strokes she needed after passing under the flags before turning or touching, but now that she thought about it, that was a count based on when she was four inches shorter. Sure, she'd done some backstroke laps in practice, but never counting with the intention of having a precise technique for competition. She'd have to go purely on instinct. How on earth was that going to work?

"One . . . two . . . three . . . four—Top Five, you got this!" Snacks screamed. She was at the end of lane two and still, her tenor soared above the rest. "Stingrays, Stingrays, Stingrays!" she called, nearly hysterical. Ellie truly had no idea how the girl still had a voice.

"Let's go," Ellie called, followed by a limp clap, her voice failing to distinguish itself among the rest.

Ellie was too jittery to properly cheer but also too jittery to stand still. She could hardly even watch. All she could think about was her next race.

Water. Maybe a sip of water would help. Was she dehydrated? She had been in that raincoat all day. Ellie scuttled to the bleachers to get a sip from her bag.

There was Joelle, crouching over her own bag, something small in her hands. She saw Ellie approaching.

"Hey, you nervous too?" Joelle asked as if reading Ellie's mind.

"How'd you know?"

"How could anyone not be nervous?"

"OMG, yes. Totally," Ellie said, relieved that she wasn't alone.

"Here, want some lavender oil?" Joelle asked. She produced a small brown vial with a purple label that reminded Ellie of a roll-on perfume. "I put it between my eyebrows. I'm sure it comes off right away in the pool, but until then it smells nice."

"I get that," Ellie said vaguely. "I'll try some."

Joelle motioned for her to come closer. Ellie bowed her head down and instinctively closed her eyes. Somehow, her charm had come out of her suit. Quickly, while Joelle dabbed the oil on her third eye, Ellie raised her hand to tuck it back in.

50-yard backstroke Ellie Greene 2nd 41.98

The flash image vanished and Ellie snapped her eyes back open. What was that? It almost seemed like the end of her would-be backstroke race visualization—a final score sheet showing a great finish with an even better time. Except she'd never gotten to the end of that visualization.

Bonkers.

"It's my ritual," Joelle said with a smile, bringing Ellie back to the present. "Lavender is very soothing, according to my terrifying stepsister."

"Uh-huh," Ellie murmured.

What was going on? The score sheet that popped into her mind's eye was hazy. Well, not hazy, but it had that azure filter. Blue hour, that's what it was. The distinct tint of Ellie's very favorite time of day.

Bonkers. Bonkers. Bonkers.

Maybe the lavender oil had gone straight to her head. But maybe not. Could lavender oil do that? What was with all these blue-tinted images popping to mind?

The announcer's voice broke through her thoughts. "Event number nine. Girls' fifty-yard backstroke!"

Ellie was up. All of a sudden, despite her rushed preparations, Ellie felt . . . ready. Readier. She had a sense that she might just pull this race off after all.

"Thanks, Joelle. I think that helped."

"You bet," Joelle said with a smile. "Good luck!"

The second Ellie jumped in the water (backstroke races started in the water, with the competitor perched against the wall, hands on the handles at the base of the block) she felt calmer than she had all meet. She let herself linger beneath the surface for a moment. That's what she loved about water. Well, about being underwater. The quiet. For just a second, the echoes and chaotic shouts from land were muffled, and it was just Ellie.

She could do this.

Ellie popped up and caught hold of the handles at the bottom of the starting block and adjusted her grip. The spot right below the dip in her collarbone burned, but again, she felt the charm's cool surface dissipate the heat. She took a big breath and let her head lean back as she exhaled, noticing the white rafters above.

"Swimmers, take your marks!"

Ellie grasped the handles of the starting block and pulled herself up out of the water, body tensed, mind focused, ready to go.

BEEP!

Without a moment's hesitation, Ellie launched, back-diving into the pool. Upon entry, the water felt like velvet against her skin. When she broke back through the surface, faceup, the cheers sounded louder than in earlier races. Splashes from lanes four and six danced into view, but Ellie didn't worry about them. Right, left, right, left. Her neck started to ache, but Ellie pressed onward, eyes trained on the ceiling the entire time, brain turned off, muscles turned on. For fifty yards, transition included, Ellie swam as fast as she possibly could.

Chapter five

"Anything you want, on the house!" the owner of Pies Only, aka Top Five's mom aka Mrs. James, called as the Stingrays piled into a long table in the back. They were there to celebrate. That's right: celebrate. The Stingrays had won. The meet had been closer than Ellie realized when going into her last race. Had she not placed second (behind Brianna), they wouldn't have gotten the extra points that bolstered their momentum going into the final IM relay. Ellie had totally bombed her butterfly race, but her individual freestyle and free relay were okay—a tiny bit faster than she'd been swimming in practice. Her random triumph in the backstroke race sort of made up for the others. Sort of. Anyway, they'd won! The Stingrays had won. After a tasteful—though almost over-the-top—pool deck celebration, Mrs. James invited the Stingrays to Pies Only to celebrate.

"The team that wins together, pies together!" Top Five exclaimed.

"Pies before goodbyes!" Snacks whooped as she opened a bag of mini pretzels.

The whole team came. Even Coach Puma joined, which was both exciting and sort of nerve-racking because it was always disorienting to see coaches or teachers or just general school grown-ups in the wild. She sat at the end of the long table with Ellie's mom and a few other parents.

Pies weren't the only "only" at the café. Everything, and Ellie meant *everything*, from floor to walls to plates to cups to all the trim between, in Pies Only was sunshine yellow. Talk about monochrome. Also, very on brand for the Stingrays. Ellie and her mom lived in the other direction, so they didn't go on their own much, but Ellie'd been for a few swim-related festivities over the years. Pies Only had one of the better vibes around. The surplus of yellow was somehow welcoming and not annoying, and the pies were delicious. Anything that was sweet and could come in pie form, they served. Once, as a special, they had a frozen lemonade pie, which Ellie found particularly inventive and refreshing.

Ellie slid into the booth at the end closest to the door, near the Tornado Girls, Tyanna, Snacks, and Top Five just as the server arrived to take orders.

"Cherry, please!" Snacks called.

"Chocolate caramel!" Tyanna added in unison.

"No way we're not getting some banana cream!" Top Five advised.

Ellie ordered a slice of blueberry peach.

While they waited for pie, snippets of conversation circulated around Ellie like air from a fan. Ellie wasn't quite sure where to insert herself. She thought to congratulate Tani, one of the Tornado Girls, who totally destroyed the competition in her freestyle race, but she was busy whispering with the other Tornados, and Ellie didn't want to interrupt; the conversation seemed pretty private. Hamburger Mike, who'd strolled over to the Tyanna duo, was talking about the correlation between hamburgers, tacos, and his mustache, which didn't really intrigue her one bit. Ellie hadn't spent much time with her teammates outside of practice this year, she realized. Similar to so many water breaks, Ellie found herself wishing she were in the pool instead of on land, swimming an easy freestyle. Before Ellie could get up and pretend to use the bathroom to kill time, Joelle slid to the open spot next to her at the end of the long booth.

"Oh, sorry, is someone sitting here?" Joelle asked, nearly jumping up, as if she'd just learned the spot was covered in fire ants.

"Oh, no, no!" Ellie exclaimed, maybe a little too loudly. "All yours!"

"Chill!" Joelle nearly shouted back, even though she was only an arm's length away. She seemed nervous. Maybe she was. "How's the pecan?"

"Pecan?" Ellie replied, confused.

"Pie? They have only pie here, right? I mean, that's what I thought the sign meant, but maybe it's like an ironic sign or something? Like a riddle. Ugh. That would be the worst. I hate riddles."

Ellie giggled. "Same. Word puzzles are basically . . ."

"A nightmare," Joelle agreed. Ellie laughed again, though she wasn't sure why. After a short pause, Joelle said, "I ordered pecan. That's my favorite." Oddly, Ellie had never had pecan pie. Come Thanksgiving, she and her mom were pumpkin devotees. "My cousin Penny makes the best pecan pie."

"Is she a chef?" Ellie asked, impressed.

"OMG, she would be so happy to hear you ask

that, but no. She's still a kid." Ellie suddenly felt like she'd maybe asked the silliest question ever. "But my other cousin Otis is. They have pet lizards."

"Cool," Ellie said, hoping her mistrust of reptiles was not apparent in her response. Then, without planning to, Ellie blurted, "I think my almost stepdad might think he is. A chef, I mean. Not a lizard."

Both girls burst into laughter. The second Ellie thought the giggle fit was over, she caught Joelle's eye, and off they went again. The thought that her mom was about to marry a man who thought he was a lizard was just too much.

Anywhere from thirty seconds to three minutes later, Snacks called Ellie's name from across the table.

"Ellie G., when's your birthday?"

Ellie wiped a tear from the corner of her eye and turned her attention to the captain. "March twentieth," Ellie answered. "Why?"

"Ahhh, makes sense. Water sign. You're very porous."

"Is that a good thing?" Ellie wasn't sure she totally understood astrology, but a good swimming-related omen couldn't hurt.

"It's a blessing and a curse, if you know what I mean."

Ellie didn't. She nodded anyway.

"Oh, and duh, you're wearing your birthstone," Joelle observed.

"What do you mean?" Ellie asked.

"Your necklace. Aquamarine."

Ellie pulled the charm off her chest to get a view, even though she knew exactly what it looked like. Huh. Maybe that's why she liked it so much. She hadn't realized the ornamentation at the top was actually her birthstone.

Bonkers.

"Hey, put in your email and I'll sign you up for the app I use. I'm sort of working on my own, but until that drops, Stargaze is the best on the market. You can friend people and it shows your compatibility and stuff."

Snacks handed Ellie her phone, and Ellie typed her email into the subscribe field.

"Joelle, what about you?" Snacks asked.

"July twenty-third," Joelle answered.

"Oh, Leo-Cancer cusp. Very potent. Complex, even."

Ellie felt her phone vibrate in her back pocket. Wow, the app people sure worked quick. She unlocked her screen and pressed the mail icon. The single unread message in her inbox looked unfamiliar at a glance.

From: YOUR FUTURE (NECKLACE)
Subject: <HEAT SHEET>

Huh. That didn't look like a message from Stargaze. Heat sheets were sometimes circulated in advance of meets, but never after. What would be the point of that? Curiosity piqued, Ellie opened the email anyway.

What Ellie discovered was unlike any heat sheet she had ever seen.

Future Necklace vs. Ellie Greene
Location: Mind's eye
Time: Blue hour
Event: Future
Heat: #1
Lane: Near future, to be exact
Time: Personal record
You've found your Future Necklace by now. That's right, the one with your birthstone on the charm. Swimmer, take your mark: The Future

Necklace will give you glimpses of the not-so-distant future. Incorporate as needed, but don't let your mind swim away so fast—it's not a fortune-teller. Simply hold the charm in your hand and close your eyes. The Future Necklace will enable you to see a flash vision of what you're ready to receive.

Ellie sat very still. As if she were underwater, the sounds around her faded away until it was just her, the necklace, and this bizarre email. Then she read it again to make sure she wasn't making anything up. Then she closed her email, logged out, and logged back in just to make sure there hadn't been some sort of internet-technology error.

There wasn't. The email remained, along with an actual welcome message from Stargaze. *Okay*, Ellie thought. *Okay, okay, okay.* She couldn't come up with words beyond that. So, she did what anyone who'd just received a mysterious email telling them the perfect, wonderful, so-cute necklace they'd found at the bottom of the pool actually had magical and potentially life-changing power would do.

She'd try it out.

Joelle and Snacks were still bantering about their sun signs, so she might as well go for it. Subtly, so her teammates wouldn't think she was falling asleep or doing anything strange, Ellie brought her right hand to her necklace and enclosed the key-shaped charm in her fist. She counted to three and closed her eyes. As promised, a blue-tinted picture appeared in her mind's eye.

Whipped cream and bright red syrup crashing onto yellow tile.

Ellie was speechless when she opened her eyes. She didn't know what the vision meant, but it was definitely a vision. Now she'd just have to wait to make sense of it. She guessed. The instructions in the email were oddly specific and vague.

"Are you into astrology stuff?" Joelle asked.

"Um." Ellie blinked, orienting herself back to the present. "I'm not sure. You?" She noticed Mrs. James and a couple of the servers emerge from the kitchen with numerous plates of pie.

"I've been known to dabble," Joelle admitted. But before Ellie could follow up, the pie arrived. Somehow, despite the chaos of a dozen-plus people ordering all different slices, the Pies Only crew got it all right. Immediately, Ellie dug into her slice of blueberry peach. Beside her, Joelle wasted no time devouring her pecan. Neither girl uttered a word. Maybe Joelle wasn't into the eating-and-talking vibe either.

"Stingrays, now that you have your pie, listen up," Coach Puma called from the head of the table. Good timing. Swimmers were less chatty when their mouths were full, Ellie observed. "Tremendous effort today. Each and every one of you. We came together. That's exactly how to start a season."

Ellie felt a swell of pride, though her terrible butterfly race still pinched. She tried to push the thought away. Looking up and down the long table, she felt happy to belong to a team. This team.

"Watch out, Riptides, here we come!" Top Five taunted. His words were met with a few whoops from across the table.

Ellie, however, felt her stomach churn. And it wasn't because she'd eaten too much pie. The Druid Hills Riptides. The biggest meet of the season, already so soon.

"The Riptides sound kinda scary," Joelle whispered.

They are, Ellie thought, though all she could manage was a nod in response. She felt the spot below her collarbone flush as if from a vicious sunburn.

What happened next seemed to occur in slow motion. A server emerged from the kitchen with an oversized slice of cherry pie under a crown of whipped cream. Top Five put his hands on the table, readying to stand. He pushed his chair back at the same moment that the server crossed behind him. Before Ellie could scream "Careful!" or "Wait!" or "Crash!" the two collided. Top Five's back hit the edge of the tray, and the pie flew through the air, more aerodynamic than Ellie ever suspected a pie slice could be; *whipped cream and bright red syrup crashed onto yellow tile, splattering everywhere.*

Bystanders jumped to their feet. Top Five profusely apologized, then ran to the kitchen to get a mop, presumably. The server managed to laugh it off, but Ellie remained frozen in her seat, eyes glued to the defunct dessert, palm over the charm dangling around her neck.

The Future Necklace was real. It was really real.

Ellie couldn't believe it. This could change, well, everything. Instantly her mind reeled, imagining a world that lacked surprises where she'd have the ultimate tool in the game of preparation (Ellie's second-favorite sport behind swimming). She took inventory of all the unexpected that had happened recently: her bummer times, the wedding announcement, and even her growth spurt. With an ability to see glimpses of the future, Ellie instantly felt steadier than she had in weeks.

Joelle murmured, "Didn't see that coming."

I did, Ellie thought.

For the first time since Ellie had grown four inches, she felt like she might be one step ahead as opposed to four steps behind.

CHAPTER SIX

Ellie's first day as a Future Necklace girl was off to an interesting start. While chewing a to-go toaster waffle on the bus to school, Ellie thought to pull out her Spanish flash cards. She had a quiz second period and was still a little rusty on some conjugations. Señor Vega's quizzes were famously tough. But Ellie had more exciting things on her mind. Why not take one peek at the future before reviewing her vocab? It would only take a second. Balancing the index cards on her lap, careful not to let them spill as the school bus careened over the sometimes-potholed streets, Ellie raised her hand to the charm. Might the jewelry show something as immediate as the end of the current bus ride? Did "not-so-distant" in this case mean the next day? Ellie didn't have to wait long to find out.

*Señor Vega writing instructions on the white-
board in blue marker:*
*Usando el tiempo pasado, describe un momento
en el que te sorprendiste recientemente.*

Ellie snapped her eyes open, thrilled with the
clarity of the picture. She could work with that.
Though she had some follow-up questions regarding
the Future Necklace heat sheet (What qualified as
"not-so-distant" future, anyway? And "ready to
receive"? That seemed a little riddle-y.), there was no
mystery surrounding what she just saw.

The Spanish quiz wasn't so much a quiz as an essay.
Much better. Señor Vega sometimes did that, shaking
it up at the last minute, but nobody ever knew when.
Until now. Great. Well, that was helpful. Ellie tucked
her index cards back into her bag. She'd long ago
committed to memory the Spanish translations for
pool, *meet*, and *victory*. She was in good shape.

Without having to worry about a quiz on the horizon, Ellie breezed through homeroom, not zoning out
once through the morning announcements.

Second-period Spanish was a delight. Usually on
quiz days Ellie spent the first part of class either

sneaking glances at her index cards or mentally running through the vocabulary list in her head. Several times she'd been called on to answer questions without a clue as to what was going on. Note-taking was out of the question. Today, however, was a different story. She dared to raise her hand to answer every question Señor Vega asked, even when she wasn't certain of the answer. When Señor Vega picked up a blue marker to write on the whiteboard, Ellie read with glee: *Usando el tiempo pasado, describe un momento en el que te sorprendiste recientemente.*

Ellie finished the assignment in record time, in the moment deciding to describe the time she saw a barracuda snorkeling in Mexico, as she already knew all the vocabulary needed for that topic too since, duh, she'd been practicing her Spanish when she was in Mexico.

She used the extra minute at the end of class to use her Future Necklace one more time. Why not? It had already been so helpful for her already! Hand clasped around the charm, Ellie inhaled deeply, held her breath at the top, closed her eyes, and exhaled.

Coach Puma walking onto the pool deck, tower of kickboards in her hands.

Whoa. Right on point. Good to know. Kick set day, coming right up. Also known as the most dreaded practice set in all of swimming, something all Stingrays agreed on. Well, at least she knew what was coming. Ellie noticed her classmates packing their book bags; the period was over. Ellie followed suit.

On her way out she passed Joelle in the hallway.

"Hey!" Ellie said. "Do you have Señor Vega for Spanish, by any chance?"

"Do these flash cards look like I have Señor Vega?" Joelle joked, but not without an eye roll that implied, *Señor Vega's vocab quizzes are the worst!*

Ellie leaned closer. "Hot tip. Quiz is canceled. Just a short essay about a time that surprised you instead."

"OMG. Sweet!" Joelle said. "Such a random topic."

"The randomest," Ellie agreed.

Joelle didn't have her own Future Necklace, but that didn't mean Ellie shouldn't share the necklace love. They might as well both enjoy the benefits!

"I'm so sore," Snacks complained, plopping down across from Ellie during lunch.

An hour earlier, Ellie's Future Necklace had showed her sitting at a table with Snacks and Top Five at lunch. When she arrived in the cafeteria, they were nowhere in sight, so she just found the nearest empty table and figured the future would work itself out. After a few minutes, she'd started to wonder if she was supposed to find them or if the vision was wrong, but as Ellie was coming to trust, the Future Necklace didn't make mistakes.

"If Puma makes us do kick sets," Top Five moaned a step behind his co-captain. He took the other seat across the table. "I don't know what I'm going to do. Well, I'll probably just do them. But ughhhh, nooooo!"

"Hate to break it to you, but it's definitely kick set day," Ellie said without thinking.

"Really? How do you know? You talk to Puma or something?" Top Five asked.

Uh-oh. How could she explain how she knew that? Ellie thought quick, backtracking. "Um . . . something like that. She sort of mentioned it slash I saw it on her clipboard that one time."

"Oh," Top Five said. Her explanation had confused him. She could tell. Before he could question her logic, Snacks intervened.

"I got extra potassium for us, then," Snacks announced, dropping a Tupperware full of balls that looked like unbaked chocolate-oatmeal cookie dough onto the table. "Eat up."

"What are these?" Ellie asked.

"She's been making them all season," Top Five explained. "You haven't had one yet?"

No, Ellie had not. She also hadn't sat with them during lunch all season, she realized.

"Yo, Joelle, Snacks got some team snacks. Eat up," Top Five called as Joelle was about to pass with a caf-eteria tray. Ellie wondered where she was going. Did she have a group of friends not on the swim team? Unclear.

Joelle set her tray down next to Ellie's.

"Potassium zone," Snacks announced, dropping one of the dough things on Joelle's tray. Joelle gave Ellie a look that seemed to ask, *What on earth is in this?*

Ellie covered her mouth as she giggled, and the second Snacks was out of earshot, already pushing her potassium balls onto Tyanna, who somehow man-aged to hold hands and carry their trays at the same time, she whispered, "They're good. Mostly dates and peanut butter, I think."

"Thank you," Joelle whispered back, before popping the whole thing in her mouth. "Does peanut butter even have potassium?"

"Good point," Ellie said. "No, I don't think so?"

"Huh."

Joelle chewed and hovered by Ellie's now-empty table. Snacks and Top Five had butterflied on.

"You can—"

"Is it—"

The two spoke over each other, their words colliding in midair.

"You go!" Ellie insisted. "Sorry!"

"No! Sorry! Was just going to say, can I—"

"Yes, sit!" Ellie said, finishing what she hoped was going to be the end of Joelle's sentence.

Joelle did. Four sort of awkward seconds later, Joelle said, "Thanks for the Spanish intel, by the way. Lifesaver."

"You bet," Ellie said with a grin, so happy to be able to help her teammate out.

"Oh, so I friended you on Stargaze," Joelle added. "You don't have to accept or anything, like, if you're not into horoscopes and stuff. But it's kinda fun. You just have to hit the little button below to friend me back."

"Okay, for sure!" Ellie exclaimed, maybe too excitedly, opening the app on her phone. "Honestly, though, I don't really know much about this stuff."

"Right. I mean, some people think it's a way to tell the future, which would be cool."

"So cool," Ellie said, feeling a tiny part sheepish that she actually did have a way to tell the future.

"But I think of it as just a way to organize or inform how you approach problems or challenges. Like a little guidebook."

"Oh, cool," Ellie said, twirling the key-shaped charm around her index finger.

"My stepsister, Zarah, got me into it. She's basically frightening in every way, mainly because she's sixteen and keeps stealing my socks from the laundry. This was the first thing she was nice about after her mom married my dad, and we became this official family and had to move here from Fanita Hills."

An official family. Move. Stepsister. Ellie had questions. Lots of questions

When did they get married? How long did it take to feel like a family? Did this Zarah girl cook lasagna and donuts that were delicious but also annoying for no obvious reason?

"You know what I mean?" Joelle asked.

Ellie didn't. She truly didn't. She'd done that thing where she zoned out again.

"Sorry, I zone out sometimes," Ellie admitted.

"Oh, me too. Like, so much. Zarah always talks about living in the present, which is nice and all, but easier said than done, if you ask me."

Ellie smiled, relieved that Joelle wasn't offended. They chatted some more, a bit about the difference between visualization and classic meditation, before exchanging phone numbers in case any Stargaze or swim stuff came up. Ellie wanted to ask her at least one of her burning questions, but lunch was over. Another time. Maybe in the future.

"Okay, see you at practice!" Joelle squeaked.

"Okay, bye, see you there!" Ellie said, with bountiful enthusiasm.

As Ellie walked through the crowded middle school halls to her next class, there was one word she couldn't get out of her mind.

Friend.

If she and Joelle were friends on Stargaze, did that

mean that they were also friends in real life? Ellie sure hoped so.

"Without further ado, kick set time," Coach Puma announced, walking onto the pool deck with a stack of kickboards impossibly balanced in her hands. Ellie had been lounging on the bleachers, listening to Snacks and Top Five discuss potential team outfit possibilities as she stretched out her quads. "Let's go. You all know what to do."

Ellie's teammates groaned. Ellie commiserated along with them, though she'd been mentally preparing for this moment all day. The experience of finally living the vision from the Future Necklace was so satisfying that she had to conceal a grin.

"It's just so. Much. Kicking!" Snacks wailed as she staggered to the edge of the pool, imitating the body language of a zombie. "Push me in, Top Five. Otherwise, I'll never."

The last time they'd done a kick set was during the week of preseason. Everyone complained about it just the same then, but at the time, Ellie hadn't minded. She was grateful for a long workout because it took up practice time with actual swimming, and more time swimming meant less time in transition. Now, though, just a couple of weeks later, it felt sort of nice to commiserate with her teammates, even if in truth she wasn't so bothered by the drill.

"Ugh," she groaned to nobody in particular. "Hope this goes quickly."

Next to her, the Tornado Girls muttered in agreement.

Ellie picked up a kickboard and jumped into the pool. This fresh camaraderie made her want to train her very hardest. Ellie kicked and kicked until her legs were mush.

At the end of the grueling set, Coach Puma called for a water break. Ellie dragged herself out of the pool and toward the bleachers to get her water bottle. Her body was so tired she wasn't sure she could bring the receptacle to her mouth to drink, much less worry about who to talk to during stretches. She stood between the mats and the bleachers, chugging.

"You were so right, Elbow Pad," Top Five said, collapsing by her feet on the stretch mat.

Ellie grinned to herself. *Elbow Pad.* Nobody had ever thought to call her that before. Ellie wasn't sure if it fit, but it was something. She thought to sit next to Top Five, but hesitated. She usually took her water breaks standing up. Gingerly, Ellie crouched down, only to stand right back up when Coach Puma called her name.

"I was blown away by your backstroke race the other day," Coach Puma said when Ellie met her by the starting blocks.

"Oh, thanks," Ellie replied. The compliment took her by surprise. Often when Coach Puma called her over for a talk, it was about a correction of some sort.

"I'm going to put you in the backstroke lanes this week during practice. We'll do time trials again before the next meet."

"Okay." What else could Ellie say? Part of her was glad that Coach Puma thought she was doing a good job, but she wanted to swim butterfly. Why couldn't she get a shot at that? Would Ellie ever get a chance? She felt the spot below her collarbone flush, only to be cooled by the surface of the charm tucked beneath her suit. Maybe, when the time came, her Future Necklace would give her a heads-up.

"You seem much more relaxed today than you have been," Coach Puma said with a slight smile, which, as far as Coach Puma's range of facial expressions went, was a major victory. In two years and counting, Ellie had seen the woman smile with her teeth only once. "Less distracted. Present. Your endurance during that set was impressive. Did you warm up differently?"

Ellie thought for a minute about how to answer the question. She stole a glance down at her necklace.

"I did," she answered truthfully, though her adjustment probably wasn't anything Coach Puma could ever have imagined.

Chapter Seven

Later that evening, Ellie sat at the kitchen counter making flash cards for geometry class. The playlist she had on—a weird old mix of her mom's from her high school days featuring one too many Boys Jump! tunes—came to an end. As if on cue, a text popped up from Joelle.

Not to be super Leo-y about it (jk), here's this playlist I made if you want to check it out. Good for kick set recovery :)))

Ellie opened the link. All songs by a band called Hat Girls. Ellie had never heard of them, but they were boppy and fun and sort of just right. *Way to know my mind*, she thought, before shooting a text back to thank her. She kept the playlist on high volume.

A few songs later, Ellie's mom walked in the front door.

"Burritos!" she called from down the hallway.

"Burritos!" Ellie repeated, springing up, right as Joelle texted her back.

Zarah loves the Hat Girls too. Literally the only thing we agree on.

Well, at least she has good taste in music, Ellie replied. Then she added an electric guitar emoji. And then, to keep things fun, the emoji of the two girls dancing in unison. Too much? She meant to imply the emoji to be Joelle and Zarah. But, actually, it could have been her and Joelle. Except not really, because Ellie was a full head taller than her teammate, and the girls in the emoji were the same height.

Ellie's mom breezed into the kitchen, interrupting Ellie's mental tangent.

"I went out on a limb and got one Cali style and the other with extra guacamole," she announced, which actually meant that she just got what they always got.

"Does Andy have a secret daughter that we don't know about?" Ellie asked as casually as possible, taking the burrito marked CALI out of the bag.

"Not that I know of," Ellie's mom answered. Without bothering to sit, Ellie unpeeled the foil from one end and took a giant bite. Delish.

"That you know of?" If Ellie's hands hadn't been occupied, she would have used her Future Necklace right then and there. Though she didn't have control over what vision the jewelry showed, if her stepdad-to-be had a daughter who would soon become her stepsister, that definitely qualified as information she was "ready to receive."

"He doesn't."

"Phew," Ellie sighed through a mouthful of beans, cheese, and sour cream. "Teenagers, ya know?"

"Sure," her mom agreed, forking a bit of chicken and guac from the center of her burrito. They remained standing at the kitchen island. Ellie knew that most people considered chairs an essential element of a meal, but when the Greene ladies were hungry, sitting fell by the wayside. They'd stood and eaten for as long as Ellie could remember. It was fun for reasons she couldn't really explain.

"What band is this?" Ellie's mom asked. "They're good."

"Aren't they?" Ellie exclaimed, an individual grain of rice flying from her mouth and onto the to-go bag. "Joelle told me about them."

"Joelle's your friend from swimming?"

Ellie paused to consider the question. Friend from swimming.

"Yes, she's my friend. New friend," Ellie explained, hopefully not jinxing anything. Would Joelle describe Ellie as her friend? Was it too soon for that? Maybe they were just teammates. But did just teammates send teammates kick set recovery playlists or share Future Necklace intel? Probably not . . .

"Did you hear what I said?"

"Huh? Yeah. Sorry. I mean, no, I didn't." Ellie pulled a soggy french fry from her burrito. It was covered in salsa and sour cream and perfect. She plopped the whole thing in her mouth. "So the jazz. Was that Andy's idea?"

Ellie's mom chewed before answering. "I wasn't the biggest fan at first," she admitted. "But it's growing on me."

Ellie nodded and ate another fry. *What was Andy's burrito order?* she wondered. She'd find out once he moved in, if not before.

The inevitable move-in. Ellie wanted to use her Future Necklace to help with that whole situation, but she had a feeling the event was still too far in the future, out of range. And even if she could get a pre-view vision showing the new layout of their living room or the kitchen with all the pots and pans and specialty cooking tools Andy inevitably owned, would that be enough? So far, the Future Necklace had shown some super-helpful images, but it hadn't assisted with explaining exactly what something might feel like. Ellie suspected that the actual experience of living with someone new would provoke surprises beyond apartment layout and decor.

Transitions.

"Hey," Ellie's mom said, setting her burrito down on the counter and wiping her mouth. "Are those flash cards for something tomorrow?"

"Pre-preparing," Ellie began. "Just flash-carding the notes I took today in class."

"How did my girl get so disciplined?" Ellie's mom asked. Ellie shrugged in response. "How about this: These burritos are delicious. But they'd probably be at least three times more delicious paired with a little *Fanplex*. What do ya say?"

"Definitely," Ellie agreed. "Probably four times."

"Season one?" Ellie's mom suggested with an eye-brow wiggle.

"I get the comfy spot!" Ellie called, racing to the TV room, claiming the part of the L-shaped sofa where she could put her legs up.

Fanplex Blues was their absolute favorite show. A cult hit from a million (okay, thirty) years ago. There were five seasons total. Together and independently, they'd seen every episode at least four times, but they hadn't started the series from the beginning in a while, usually opting for a random one here and there.

Sometimes it was easier to talk about serious things if you were doing something else. The multi-tasking syndrome. Ellie witnessed it the first time when her parents told her they were getting divorced. She still remembered that her dad had been unload-ing the dishwasher the entire time and her mom had been knitting (a very short-lived hobby they now laughed openly about). At the time, Ellie wondered why they couldn't sit still, since she was perched on a kitchen stool with her legs crossed, holding her breath, frozen in place.

But sometimes it was just easier to do something

else. Ellie had more questions for her mom about Andy, thoughts that threatened to swirl through Ellie's head as her mom dug under the couch cushion for the remote.

Ellie thought to use her Future Necklace, but the impulse passed. What did she need to see the future for when the present was this good? Currently, Ellie was content. She had a part of a burrito in her belly, part of a burrito in her hand, and at least an hour of dynamic (not to mention melodramatic) television in front of her. She didn't want to miss a moment.

Chapter Eight

"Okay, so, we're sort of low on snacks because grocery day isn't until tomorrow, but I think we have some leftover pizza if you're hungry," Ellie rambled as she unlocked the front door to her apartment.

"Oh, I'm good," Joelle said, one step behind her.

"You don't have to take your shoes off or anything if you don't want to," Ellie explained.

"Okay, cool." Joelle took off her slip-on sneakers anyway. "Sorry. Zarah is obsessed with not having street germs inside, so I'm kind of used to it. Not that the other way is wrong or anything. Just habit."

"Totally." Ellie bent down to unlace her high-tops. She didn't want to be a bad host, and maybe that meant not wearing shoes. Ellie wasn't sure, to be honest. She noted the absence of her mom's purse on the hook on the wall. Ellie wasn't used to being home so early in the afternoon. The apartment was both quiet and bright with mid-afternoon desert rays.

It had seemed like a good idea to invite Joelle over after school. A great idea, even. Ellie's Future Necklace didn't show her that swim practice was canceled—the news came from Coach Puma through Joelle during lunch. Rumor had it that a package of frozen chicken patties clogged up and then broke the pool filters. Coach Puma told Snacks to tell everyone to rest up and that they'd reconvene tomorrow with time trials before their upcoming Saturday meet.

Ellie had used her Future Necklace to see if she could get a glimpse of the trials. No such luck. Instead, she saw a picture of Joelle's giant red swim bag by the front door of her apartment by the coatrack. Which obviously meant that Joelle would be coming over to Ellie's place. That, or Ellie was to steal Joelle's swim bag and bring it home, which seemed a much less reasonable explanation.

Just at that moment, Joelle had caught her eye and admitted, "I was so looking forward to being in a pool today."

"Come over," Ellie had replied without thinking. "I have a pool at my apartment complex!"

And that had been that. Until Ellie started worrying on the bus ride home, not about anything in particular, but about all sorts of things. So, yeah. Maybe it hadn't been such a good idea after all. Now that the hang was happening, things felt awkward and weird.

Ellie dropped her bags by the front door. Joelle did the same.

"Should I change into my suit up here?" Joelle asked.

"Oh, yes. Good idea."

Joelle got her suit from her bag, and Ellie showed her to the bathroom. Then she ran to the kitchen to see if there was anything less weird than old pizza as a snack. She found a rogue package of gummy bears and a half-eaten box of crackers. Before Joelle made it back out, Ellie checked her Future Necklace real quick. Maybe there would be another clue about the afternoon ahead. Already, this impromptu non-practice pool hang felt riddled with unpredictability.

Ellie wrapped her fingers around the charm and

closed her eyes. Like clockwork, a blue-tinted vision popped into her mind:

Andy standing over the stove in the kitchen, stirring a nearly overflowing pot, wearing a red apron.

Huh. Okay. Not super helpful as far as her hang with Joelle went, but still useful enough nonetheless. The Future Necklace sure would be more thorough if it came with timestamps or something. The "not-so-distant" part sort of clarified it, but sort of didn't. Was Andy making dinner that night or the next? Ellie really wasn't in the mood to make small talk with her future stepdad that evening. She probably wouldn't the next either. At least she had a heads-up.

"Ready?" Joelle said, popping back into the kitchen.

"Oh, do you like crackers?"

"They're okay, I guess." Joelle stood there, sort of in between the kitchen island and the kitchen table. No-man's-land. She looked at the floor. Ellie didn't know what to do. Were crackers annoying in a way she hadn't realized?

This was awkward. Why was this awkward? They

were friends now, weren't they? They'd texted that one time about the playlist. They'd talked on the bus and during a water break the other day. Maybe Ellie had interpreted the vision from the necklace incorrectly. Maybe Joelle wasn't destined to come over after all. Maybe Ellie had interpreted it all wrong!

Standing there in her own kitchen, Ellie suddenly felt taller than she'd ever felt.

"To the pool?" Joelle suggested, breaking through the fog of worries gathering in Ellie's brain.

"Let's do it," Ellie replied, relieved Joelle had taken the reins.

"OMG, your pool has a diving board?" Joelle exclaimed, dropping her towel on the nearest lounge chair. Ellie waved to the afternoon lifeguard on duty, who sat bored, sunburned, and twirling her whistle lanyard on a chair by the shallow end, and kicked off her slides. Without any warning or even testing the water temperature with her toe, Joelle skipped to the diving board, took a running start, and performed the most thrilling front flip Ellie had ever seen outside of the televised Olympics.

"How did you do that?" Ellie asked when Joelle surfaced.

"Years of practice," Joelle answered, swimming to the ladder.

"Really?" Ellie said, slightly disappointed.

"No, I'm kidding. I'll show you."

So Ellie and Joelle spent the next hour doing diving-board tricks. Turned out a front flip wasn't all that Joelle had in her arsenal. She could also backflip and had an extremely elegant swan dive.

"I give that an eight," Ellie called after Joelle took her stab at a cannonball. "The splash could have been a little more even," she teased.

"Psshhh." Joelle rolled her eyes, but in a way that felt very friendly and not rude.

Ellie showed Joelle her specialty, which just so happened to be a pencil jump. Now that she was so darn tall, the simple move sort of packed a punch. With the intention of creating as little splash as possible, Ellie sprang off the end of the board and glided into the water at a 90-degree angle with her arms pressed to her sides, legs together, toes pointed. She entered the water like a nail, shooting to the bottom of the deep end, feet grazing the pool floor, probably not all that far away from where she'd discovered her Future Necklace not even a week earlier.

"A perfect ten! I can't believe it! Ellie Greene has scored a perfect ten!" Joelle cheered when Ellie surfaced. Ellie laughed and blew kisses to an imaginary crowd of fans.

A few pencil-cannons later (a hybrid move that the girls invented and just could not get enough of), Joelle said, "Okay, you're warmed up. Ready for the flip?"

Ellie wasn't so sure. She'd never tried one before. What if she landed on her face? Or, more likely, her back? That sounded . . . bad. Nevertheless, she followed Joelle out of the pool.

"Okay, this is the trick: You have to run up to the end, and right when you jump, pretend you're throwing a ball over your head. Like, you're trying to throw it really far." Joelle demonstrated on the side of the pool. "So when you start to flip forward, the motion propels you to rotate faster."

Ellie mimed the movement a few times. "Like this?"

"Exactly," Joelle confirmed. "Like a throw-in in soccer. Which is a sport I've never watched, but that's what Zarah says. She taught me."

Ellie didn't know much about throw-ins either, but she did her best to mimic Joelle's demonstration.

"Wanna try?" Joelle invited her, a little glimmer in her eye.

Ellie hesitated. "I'm not sure. I don't quite know what's going to happen . . ."

"Of course you don't. But why not try?"

So Ellie did.

She stepped up onto the diving board, lingering at the back for a moment. The bumpies beneath her feet felt just like the top of a starting block. Her collarbone spot burned. Ellie felt the charm press against her skin beneath her bathing suit. The silver had a cooling effect.

"You got this," Joelle called from the side of the pool.

Ellie galloped to the end of the board. Two steps from the back, she brought her hands up and back over her head. She shuffled her feet at the end, then took one jump to spring, and launched herself forward off the board.

A second later, when she landed on her back, it didn't sting nearly as much as she would have expected.

Joelle looked worried when Ellie surfaced, but

once Ellie burst out laughing, it was all over. By the time their hysterics had subsided, Ellie would have sworn their happy tears could have added at least an inch to the level of pool water.

"It's actually sorta like the two-hand touch," Ellie noted once they'd finally caught their breath. "The part where you throw your hands over your head, I mean."

"Huh. I never thought of it that way, but you're sorta right," Joelle agreed.

Ellie swam to the middle of the pool to give herself a few strokes into the turn. It was wonky, because with a pool shaped like a kidney bean, no side was perfectly straight, but she tried anyway, starting from the middle of the pool. She took a few strokes, then envisioned she was about to flip on the diving board as she came to the wall. The motion was for sure different, but something about doing the flip instead of the two-hand touch made it somewhere between a gazillion and four bajillion times easier.

"That looked perfect," Joelle called from the side.

Ellie tried again. It felt even better now. Huh. Who would have thought that practicing front flips might teach her something about butterfly?

"Coach Puma is tough, don't ya think?" Joelle asked a few minutes later. Golden hour was fading into blue, and the verdin were out. Ellie had counted four already. The girls floated next to each other on their backs, their legs over the edge, anchoring them to the side.

"She's . . . how to put it . . ."

"Serious," Joelle offered, taking the word right out of Ellie's mouth.

"Yeah." Then, without planning to, Ellie admitted, "I was really hoping she'd put me on the IM relay team this year. I don't have a chance at free because I'm pretty sure Brianna's got that on lock, but for fly. My times have been so off this season, though."

"You'll get there. You have time," Joelle encouraged. "At least you've been getting off the block okay. I don't know if you've noticed, but I've been a full cement statue up there. At least in the last meet."

Ellie hadn't noticed.

"It's probably more in your head than you think," Ellie said, repeating something she'd heard Snacks say to Top Five once last season when he'd been worried about his breathing technique being weird, despite no evidence of the sort. "And hey, worst case, you can just do a front flip into the water."

Joelle laughed. "Probably worth the DQ."

"Look, if you're gonna DQ, do it in style," Ellie joked.

The two floated and chatted until not only their fingertips pruned but also their earlobes and belly buttons (if that was a thing). Joelle told Ellie stories about that band the Hat Girls, and how she once saw them perform at a Battle of the Bands competition. Ellie told the story of how she almost choked on a (delicious) lasagna noodle when her mom and Andy spilled the engagement beans, which led to a rabbit hole of stories about visits gone wrong at the zoo, of which, surprisingly, they each had quite a few. The blue hour was in full effect when Ellie's mom, evidently having arrived home from work while the girls were diving, called out from the terrace.

"Hey, Prunies!" she shouted, using her standard greeting for when Ellie stayed in the pool too long. "Joelle's dad is here! Ellie, dinner's almost ready!"

Ellie and Joelle peeled themselves out of the pool to dry off.

"How long did it take to get used to having family

dinners with people that don't feel like your family yet?" Ellie asked, remembering the vision of Andy cooking, wrapping a towel around her shoulders.

Joelle thought for a second. "Well, they've been married for a year now, so . . . I dunno. My stepmom is totally normal and nice. Zarah is weird but mostly nice. Just a little unpredictable. I think the thing that took the longest to get used to was seeing grown-up woman and teenager clothes in the laundry room."

"Interesting." Ellie had never thought about that before, but worth considering for when Andy moved in. Whenever that would be.

"Is this stepdad person a sock stealer, you think?" Joelle asked.

"Can't tell," Ellie said. "Probably not?" Andy seemed way too polite for that, actually. "So how do I get out of dinner with them?"

"Blame it on an assignment for health class. And keep it vague," Joelle offered. "If Andy's anything like my dad, he won't ask, and your mom won't push it."

The girls arrived in the kitchen to get Joelle's swim bags. Andy stood at the counter just as the

Future Necklace predicted, tears rolling down his cheeks. She hadn't seen that Andy would be crying. Maybe Ellie hadn't paid close enough attention to the vision. Though, to be fair, he was also cutting onions.

"Hey, girls." He sniffled. "Don't mind me."

Ellie looked away. She didn't like to look at kids when they cried. Seeing a grown-up cry was even weirder. Even if it was onion related. Ellie had never tried to chop one of the things, but she'd heard stories.

"Hi, I'm Joelle. It's nice to meet you," Joelle said, waving.

"I'm Andy."

Oh. So that really was what she should call him. Good to know.

"Want to stay for dinner?" Andy asked. "I'm making my chili. I promise the waterworks will be over in a second."

"Joelle probably has to go home," Ellie excused, annoyed that Andy had brought it up. What if she didn't like chili or thought onions were too emotional of a vegetable to eat? Ellie was sort of starting to think the same thing herself.

"I love chili," Joelle said. "But my dad's already here to pick me up."

"Next time," Andy said with a smile. Ellie noticed that his forehead looked less shiny than usual.

"Next time!" Joelle chirped. Ellie smiled to herself, happy that both Andy and Joelle thought that she'd be over again.

Ellie walked Joelle out. Her mom was already outside chatting it up with Joelle's dad.

"Hey, Ellie," Andy called from the kitchen when she returned. "Do you know where the soup pot is?"

"Soup pot?" Ellie asked, stifling a laugh. She didn't know there was such a specific kind of pot.

"Yeah, something a little bigger than this one," he said, gesturing to the big-enough-looking pot on the stove. That was what they always used to reheat ramen or cooked canned soup in. Ellie told him as much.

"Okay, this will do!" Andy sure was chipper. She'd never seen someone so excited about a pot.

Ellie wished she could see way more into the future. Learning of the occasional pop quiz and swim drill were nice and all, but they didn't answer some of the bigger questions. What would it be like with Andy living in their house? What would it be like at her mom's wedding? Nothing to do but wait and find out. Actually, nothing to do except wait until those events were in the not-so-distant future.

As planned, Ellie ate dinner in her room. Thanks to Joelle (and her Future Necklace, let's be honest), she'd convinced her mom and Andy that her assignment for health class was worth half her grade and she really needed to prepare. She'd gone back to her geometry flash cards for a minute, but instead fell into her usual pattern of watching old Olympics on YouTube. Inspired by her afternoon, she watched mostly diving competitions, for once.

Were she and Joelle on the road to becoming best friends? Okay, maybe that was too much. Good friends? It sorta seemed like it! Ellie had never had a best friend who was also a teammate. If they did become best friends, they could of course do normal best friend stuff like sleepovers and all-night *Fanplex* marathons (hopefully, Joelle loved the show as much as she did). Now that Joelle had met her mom and Andy, maybe she'd invite Ellie over to hang out. The infamous Zarah probably wasn't as scary as Joelle made her seem, but if she was, then they could commiserate about it together. But as swim team best friends, they could also maybe carpool to meets sometimes and practice together on their own and share goggles and caps (not suits—Ellie was a solid six inches taller) and—

The possibilities felt almost limitless. Ellie let herself daydream about all the exciting ways a swim team best friendship might unfold.

After a while, Ellie had worked up a whole other appetite. When she wandered out to the kitchen for seconds, Ellie overheard the TV from the next room. *Fanplex Blues* was on. The episode where Mandy and Leila borrow their mom's car and drive to the beach for the weekend. It was her favorite episode. Man. If she'd known they'd be watching the best episode of the best show ever, she wouldn't have fibbed about the homework. Sort of too late now to go back on it. Ellie scooped herself another bowl of chili and shuffled to her bedroom.

On her way, she passed the hallway that led to the apartment's entrance. A flash of red in her periphery caught her attention. There by the front door and the coatrack sat Joelle's ruby-red swim bag. Ellie smiled, thought once again of the feeling of soaring through the air (pre-backflop). The Future Necklace had worked to her advantage after all. Without seeing the glimpse of Joelle's swim bag, she might never have had the courage to invite Joelle over to begin with. Ellie gave her charm a loving squeeze, before texting her new friend about her bag, left behind but not lost.

Chapter Nine

Ellie's Future Necklace instructions should have come with fine print. Or finer print. Or maybe bold print. Some kind of print that warned the necklace wearer that sometimes they might see something they didn't particularly want to see, and even though the warning would be helpful, maybe seeing that vision would still throw them off. That person, in this case being Ellie, and that vision, being the one she'd seen just prior to the start of swim practice in which a big cardboard box sat inside their front door with the word KITCHEN written on the side in large black block letters. It was the kind of box that really could mean only one thing.

Someone was moving. And it didn't take a rocket scientist or a Future Necklace to infer that the box belonged to Andy.

Andy was moving in. Starting to move in, at least. Sometime in the not-so-distant future.

Ellie had used her Future Necklace just before swim practice, quickly, in the corner of the locker room after changing into her suit, to see if she could get any intel on the upcoming time trials. *Why not?* she'd thought. This was not what she'd been hoping for. Afterward, she'd rushed out to the pool deck in an effort to get a moment of peace and quiet to maybe do a visualization before the others joined, but all she could do was stew in her thoughts. Her mouth suddenly tasted like cereal milk, but in the bad way, like if you waited too long to brush your teeth after devouring two bowls of the sugary kind first thing in the morning.

Was Andy just going to move in gradually, box by box? Or was the vision incomplete—just indicating one of many cardboard cubes she'd find upon her return to the apartment sometime soon . . . in the near future? And what was with this whole "near future" thing anyway? Sure, all the visions so far had come to pass within the same day (or if at night, the next morning), but still. There was a lot of variability in there. Ellie had a mind to send the Future Necklace creators some notes, if she could ever find out who they were.

The patch of skin beneath her charm sizzled. Ellie sat on the bleachers on the pool deck glumly. She didn't notice that her teammates had gathered around until Coach Puma started with instructions for that day's practice.

"Time trials," Coach Puma began as Joelle plopped down right next to Ellie. The girls shared a quick smile. They knew better than to interrupt Coach Puma when she was doling out instructions. "This isn't supposed to be stressful."

Why didn't coaches and teachers and authority figures in general understand that if they tell kids something isn't supposed to be stressful, then it automatically becomes stressful? From the way Joelle's back stiffened and her fingers started to wiggle like alive spaghetti, Ellie suspected she felt the same way.

"Now that the season has officially begun, this just serves as an assessment so you know where you're at, what you need to work on. They'll also inform how I build the lineup for the next meet against the Barracudas on Saturday."

Saturday. That was a few days away. Would Andy be all the way moved in by then? What kind of kitchen stuff did he have, anyway? Hopefully, an adequate soup pot. Ellie would have to clarify how she'd organized the kitchen cabinets before he unpacked. He better not disrupt her system. She'd been very considerate when she and her mom moved in.

"We're going to do this in pairs," Coach Puma explained.

"Partners?" Joelle whispered, nudging Ellie's arm.

"Duh," Ellie mouthed back.

Coach Puma explained that each pair would receive a stopwatch, every swimmer responsible for taking and recording the times for their partners. Every swimmer would swim each race—fifty free, fifty fly, fifty breast, and fifty back.

"Transitions—not just in the pool but between heats—are key. No horsing around. Get stretched and then to your lanes. Everybody is going to test on everything. This is low-key, all right? Do your best but have fun."

Ellie's teammates murmured in agreement, though what Ellie heard loudest was her internal monologue: *This is your shot to blow your bad times out of the water and earn a spot on the IM relay! Now or never! Your last chance at glory, your best chance at grace . . .*

Time trials only to return home to Andy's boxes? This was proving to be the worst day ever.

Ellie felt a nudge on her shoulder.

"You good?" Joelle asked.

Ellie nodded.

"Don't worry, we got this. Front flip style. That two-hand touch's got nothing on you."

Joelle was right. Ellie was prepared. As prepared as she could be. She'd practiced in practice, outside of practice, and now all she had to do was swim.

And she had a friend who knew exactly what to say, no Future Necklace required.

Ellie felt a little better. A lot better, actually. Time to get her head in the game. She could think about Andy and his boxes—plural, singular, whatever they might be—later. She could also worry about her times later. Maybe she wouldn't even have to worry. At present, she had some swimming to do.

The team warmed up and assembled into their lanes. Ellie and Joelle, along with a sixth-and-eighth-grade duo, took lane two. They'd rotate through the four strokes—free, back, breast, then fly—resting while the other couples swam.

Joelle lined up on the block first. She looked nervous. Ellie knew the feeling well.

"J!" she called, right before Joelle took her mark. Ellie had never shortened her name before, but there wasn't time to think much about it. "When in doubt, front flip it," Ellie joked, clapping her hands together. A huge smile appeared on Joelle's face, and Ellie thought she saw her friend's shoulders drop in relief.

Even though the time trials weren't a real meet, and even though they were "low-key," when Coach Puma's whistle blew, Ellie shouted and cheered and screamed for Joelle. Her voice, along with her teammates' voices, filled every inch of air above the surface of the pool.

In a twist Ellie could have never predicted, the time trials were super fun. Not low-key in the traditional sense, but the second Joelle dove into the pool, Ellie's worries evaporated. Well, they were probably hidden deep in there somewhere, but Ellie didn't have time to dwell. If she wasn't swimming, she was cheering. If she wasn't shouting for Joelle or her other teammates to "Go, go, go," then she was in the pool herself, flying down the length of lane two from one end to the other.

Ellie managed to shave a second off her freestyle and breaststroke times, and a little over two from backstroke. Butterfly was all she had left. Joelle and Ellie double high-fived as Joelle took the block.

"Best for—"

"Last!"

The next lane over, Top Five started, "Ka—

"Pow!" Snacks finished.

Coach Puma blew her whistle, and Ellie watched Joelle, Top Five, Tye, Brianna, Hamburger Mike, and a sixth grader dive off the blocks.

Ellie wasn't sure what came over her in the next moment. She was cheering and screaming just like everyone else. Maybe it was the color of the pool water, or maybe it was when Snacks hollered, "Scorpios never give up!" that reminded Ellie of the birthstone around her neck. Either way, she thought to use the Future Necklace really quick. Usually, she hoped to get a glimpse of the future to settle something she was nervous about. Now, however, Ellie was having a blast. She was excited for what else was in store and couldn't wait for the future to happen!

As Joelle headed into the turn, Ellie dashed her hand up to her collar and closed her eyes.

Coach Puma pulling a shiny purple warm-up jacket from a bin. The word FEVER *spelled in yellow letters across the back.*

Ellie popped her eyes open, the image vanishing as the pool in front of her captured her view. She didn't have time to analyze what she'd seen. Joelle was twenty yards away from the finish.

"Let's go, almost home!" she shouted down the length of the lane, leaning over and cupping her hands around her mouth for maximum effect. No, she didn't think much about the vision, because she didn't have to. It was obvious that Coach Puma would be surprising them with the team jackets every swimmer had their hearts set on.

After the trials were complete, every single Stingray lay flopped on their backs on the stretch mats, arms wide, like a bunch of . . . well, stingrays. Ellie was panting from her final swim. Joelle was panting from screaming so loud during Ellie's final swim. Everyone else was in one boat or the other.

Ellie stared at the ceiling above. She'd done it. She'd broken her record, swum her personal best in the fifty-yard butterfly. She wasn't sure what had made the difference, exactly. Thinking about doing a front flip off a diving board into the two-hand touch transition definitely helped. She hadn't thought to pause, never considered hesitation, just sort of visualized she was about to flip and boom: transition over with. But that wasn't all. Ellie had felt at home in the water again. Her whole body—all four extra inches of it—took over, her mind completely quiet. She'd loved every second of that swim.

"Great work today, everyone," Coach Puma said. "We're in great shape going into Saturday's meet. But what I'm most impressed by is the teamwork that everyone displayed. I know many of you broke some personal records." Ellie's heart fluttered. That was her! "But the support I saw on the pool deck is what makes a team strong."

A few whoops filled the air like the final fireworks of a Fourth of July display. Coach Puma's pump-up speeches were as effective as ever. Ellie propped herself up on her elbows for a better view.

She continued, "I'm not sure if you all have covered this in biology class yet, but does anyone know what you call a group of stingrays?"

For once, not a single swimmer on the team had an immediate answer.

Coach Puma smiled. "A fever."

"Ooooh, that's tough," Top Five said under his breath.

"Hot, hot, hot," Snacks said, fanning her face with one hand before plopping a handful of fluorescent candy in her mouth. Even Hamburger Mike seemed impressed.

"What I saw today was a fever of swimmers." Everyone was very silent all of a sudden. "This is going to be a great season, because you all make a great team. I was going to wait until after the meet on Saturday, but I think a fun surprise before won't hurt."

That's when Ellie knew. The team jackets—the purple ones she saw in her Future Necklace vision. They were getting them right now.

On cue, Coach Puma dragged a bin from behind the bleachers into view. From inside, she pulled a shimmery purple jacket. It was sort of vintage in style, like an old baseball team jacket from the 1990s with the striped lining around the neck and ends of the sleeves. Coach Puma held the garment up high; across the back, in big yellow letters, it said FEVER.

The Mariposa Stingrays erupted. That was the only way to put it.

"No way!"

"Ahhhhh!"

"Siiiiick!"

"Kapow!"

"KAPOW!"

Everyone was on their feet, including Ellie, rushing to the bleachers to get theirs. Coach Puma laughed, showing all her very white teeth, as she handed them out.

"Okay, one at a time!" she said, but it was no use. She was swarmed.

Ellie slid her arms into the shimmery sleeves. It fit perfectly.

"Can you believe it? These are so cool!" Joelle said, doing a spin.

"I can't!" Ellie fibbed, because of course she could. Unlike the rest of her teammates, she hadn't been surprised by this surprise at all.

Coach Puma insisted they take an informal team picture. Ellie stood in the back row between Brianna and Joelle, arms around each of her teammates, enormous smile plastered to her face, hopefully concealing the teeny-tiny feeling that maybe she would have felt more united with her fever if she'd been as truly surprised as the rest. It wasn't that it felt like a bummer to fake it—she was still so happy to have the jacket, but she somehow felt a little left out.

Was that possible? She didn't understand why, exactly, but the information she'd gained in advance made her feel ever so slightly lonely in the moment.

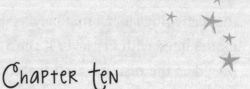

Chapter ten

By the time Ellie arrived home, her mood had re-soured. Plus, she was exhausted. Pretending to be as surprised as her teammates about the jackets on top of the time trials really took it out of her. Her swim bag and book bag hooked over each arm, Ellie leaned against the front door to push it open. It jammed against something, only yielding halfway. That's when she remembered.

The box. Andy's move-in box.

Ellie pushed the door with all her might, not caring if the items she smooshed against the wall were fragile.

"What the—" Ellie howled, stubbing her toe as she tried to squeeze through the slivered doorway. Why would anyone leave a giant box right in the doorway? Was this the kind of thing she had to look forward to when sharing a house with her mom's fiancé? Was he a total slob and they were just now finding out?

"Sorry, love, I just got home!" Ellie's mom called from somewhere inside.

Suddenly, Ellie was mad. Madder than mad. Mad that she'd stubbed her toe, mad that her feet were so big her toes were extra stub-able, mad that there was a ridiculous box in the doorway to begin with, mad that she was so tall now that it made it trickier to inch through partially obstructed doorways. The list probably went on.

Ellie's mom emerged, work skirt paired with an old T-shirt. One sock was on, one off. "I'm feeling Indian tonight. What you think?"

So Ellie told her. She told her what she thought. About everything.

"This is so unfair! His stuff is going to take over! You promised we'd talk about it but there it is! His box of stuff—probably fancy pots or whatever you need to cook all those fancy things—is going to ruin all my organization and then he's going to move more stuff in and the entire apartment is going to change and look weird and I just don't want everything to change so quickly!" Ellie paused and took a breath.

The skin surrounding her collarbone felt like it was on fire. "And! I don't want Indian food for dinner!" Suddenly, it occurred to Ellie that if Andy's box (boxes plural?) were in their house, maybe Andy was also there. Maybe she had gone too far. Ellie shouted one last thing into the air. "And, Andy—if you're here, I'm sorry. I don't think it's anything personal. This is just a lot!"

With that, Ellie collapsed on the floor, spent. She wished she could climb inside her swim bag that lay by her feet. If she were four inches shorter, she could probably fit, no problem.

Ellie's mom came and perched down on the ground right next to her. They sat like that, together in silence, for a long, long time.

"It's really not Andy's box?" Ellie asked. They stood at the kitchen island eating nachos right out of the delivery container. They'd never ordered nachos before, but El Conquistador had a special going on, so they decided to give them a shot. The nachos were . . . okay. Better than Ellie expected, but soggier than she'd hoped.

"It's really not Andrew's. I restaged a kitchen for the showing I had today," Ellie's mom explained, not for the first time.

"Okay." Now that her mom mentioned it, Ellie remembered coming home a few weeks ago to half a dozen bags filled with throw pillows, blankets, and very boring vases.

"Well, that's good," Ellie said, stuffing her mouth full with an extra-cheesy chip to buy herself some time. Ellie chewed and swallowed and then took a sip of water before she began. "I don't hate Andy, you know."

Ellie's mom said nothing.

"Really. He's nice. Maybe not *cool*," she joked, remembering his glasses, "but I think he's good. Truly good. And I know if you love him, then I'll love him too."

"I hope so, love," Ellie's mom said. "All I ask is that you give him a chance. He might surprise you."

"He might," Ellie considered. "I will. I promise."

They ate in silence for a few bites.

"How was practice?" Ellie's mom asked.

"Well . . ." Ellie began. She was trying to stay pouty, but it wasn't really working. The corners of her lips curled into an involuntary smile. "I sorta broke my PR. For butterfly."

"Sorta?!" Ellie's mom exclaimed. "That's huge! Congrats!"

"Thanks," Ellie said. It *was* huge. And almost hard to believe after all the trouble she'd had over the last few weeks. "It's been a weird start to the year."

"I know."

They ate a few more bites in silence before Ellie's mom said, "Ellie, Andrew and I are getting married. He's not moving in today, tomorrow, or even next week. We're all going to talk about it together. I promised you that. I wouldn't break that promise. I know this is a big transition."

That word was just everywhere.

"But, Ellie . . ." Her mom paused. "Andrew *is* moving in. There will be some adjustments. And some things might be hard at first. But try to be open to the possibility that it won't be all bad. Change can be hard. And not knowing what's coming can be scary."

I'll say, Ellie thought, peering down at the charm hanging from the simple silver chain.

"But let's just take it one day, one moment at a

time. Remember: It's just a hole in the ground with water in it. Okay?"

Ellie nodded.

Ellie's mom reached out her hand and placed it tenderly over her daughter's heart. Ellie didn't realize she was crying until she saw a small drop of water land on the tip of her mom's finger. They weren't sad tears, not entirely. Rather, the kind of tears that escape because there's nowhere else for your thoughts, your feelings, and for pieces of your heart to go.

After brushing her teeth, Ellie leaned her hand onto the sink and sighed. She felt better. Sort of. Even though Andy's move-in was inevitable, she was relieved that she'd finally talked about it with her mom. She trusted that it wouldn't be the complete ambush that she feared.

Give Andrew a chance.

She'd promised her mom that she would. The task sounded a little bit harder now than it had at the time.

Ellie turned on the faucet to splash some water onto her collarbone zone, which was burning up. Ellie caught the reflection of her necklace.

Had her Future Necklace led her astray? In the case of the cardboard box, it sort of had. Right? Ellie pulled up the heat sheet email with the instructions, considering them again, word for word. It still lacked some of the fine print that she craved, though one phrase that she'd forgotten about stuck out.

Incorporate as needed.

Maybe she'd been using her Future Necklace all wrong. And by all wrong, she meant not enough. Sure, the fine print she'd hoped for would have helped. And, especially in this most recent event, seeing a longer vision certainly would have been imperative. But maybe that wasn't the necklace's fault.

No, of course it wasn't. She wasn't using her Future Necklace incorrectly. She just wasn't using it enough— she *needed* to incorporate it more, *needed* to pay closer attention to the details within each vision. That was it! How could she expect her necklace to show her everything she needed to see if she was relying on it in such a limited capacity? If she had Future Necklaced again before practice, she probably would have seen that the inside of the box was all her mom's work stuff, not Andy's, and her outburst could have been avoided entirely.

Ellie brought her hand around her charm and held tight. She took a deep breath and closed her eyes.

Comforter pulled over her body, phone propped against her knees, two-hundred-meter freestyle race playing on her phone.

Satisfied, Ellie went to finish her homework. She didn't pause to consider that the Future Necklace had only revealed how Ellie fell asleep almost every night of the week.

Chapter Eleven

Ellie woke up early on meet days. That's just what she did.

But . . .

If the way to deal with change, as her mom had put it, was to take it one moment at a time, then Ellie would just go ahead and seize some extra early morning moments. Extra moments of sleep.

Ellie's alarm went off at dawn, per usual, but she was groggy and reasoned that early morning visualization might not be totally necessary. Visualization was so . . . how to put it? Hypothetical? Unreliable? Time-consuming? Anyway, why visualize when she had a literal future-telling necklace at her disposal?

So, for the first time ever on a meet day, Ellie hit snooze. Then she hit it again, and a third and final time before getting out of bed to get dressed. Snacks and Top Five had announced "cool and classy" as the team outfit theme (aka all black with their new fever jackets).

"Monochrome fever," they'd said, before warning everyone that mercury was still in retrograde.

Ellie was glad that the instructions didn't elicit too many variables. When she finally peeled herself out of bed, after using her Future Necklace to reveal a vision indicating her bus was also running late, she didn't have to think much about it before pulling on her favorite black jeans, uncuffing a fold at the bottom to make them longer, and her only black T-shirt. She wore her all-black sneakers for good measure.

Ellie kept up her Future Necklace discipline throughout the morning, starting when Ms. Bianco took attendance.

"Ellie G.?"

"I beg your pardon!" Ellie said as she retrieved her charm from under the collar of her shirt. *What would the necklace show now?* she wondered.

"Not necessary," Ms. Bianco called in reply, but Ellie wasn't listening. Instead, she was busy calculating how many more times she'd need the Future Necklace to ensure solid info pertaining to that afternoon's meet. At least once a period, she figured. She didn't want to take any chances or risk slacking off.

Her Future Necklace check before math showed the clock on the wall during Spanish class. *Ahhh, time standing still*, Ellie thought, which made perfect sense considering Señor Vega ended up lecturing the entire period about the origin of verb conjugations. Total snooze zone.

Before lunch—not Future Necklace–inspired, actually—Ellie suddenly remembered she still needed to finish her science homework. She'd planned to answer the remaining questions during their fifteen minutes of free time during homeroom, but she'd consumed most of those minutes Future Necklacing and thinking super, super carefully about what each vision meant, so as to avoid an out-of-context mix-up like the night before.

Ellie found an empty table and took out her science folder. A few minutes later, Joelle sat down across from her and began peeling an orange.

"Do you think that the Barracudas are going to, like, cheer really loud?"

"What do you mean?" Ellie replied while scribbling

down something, hopefully factual, in her notebook about wetland biodiversity.

"Well, you know how when the other team cheers really loud, especially if it's an indoor pool, it can be super distracting. Like, imagine a whole team full of Snacks," Joelle described. Then, laughing, she said, "I mean Snacks the person, not a swim team full of pretzels and chips and candy and peanut butter crackers. Though, I mean, now that I am imagining that, maybe that could be a good cartoon or something."

"Yeah, that would be annoying," Ellie murmured as she tried to think of the best way to describe the concept of watershed but also now considering how swimming against a team with over-the-top cheering capacity might get pretty distracting. And exactly the kind of thing that would be helpful to know in advance.

"Anyway, maybe I'm just nervous about the meet," Joelle admitted. "I had a dream last night that my feet were cemented to the block and I couldn't dive off until after the race had already ended."

"I hate dreams," Ellie said, though what she thought was *How can I sneak a necklace look without Joelle noticing? Would it even be that bad if she noticed? I could say I was meditating, or just thinking about . . . something.*

No, that would be weird. Maybe it's worth it?

The moment Joelle glanced down at her orange again, Ellie shut her eyes and closed her hand around the charm. Before she could take a deep breath, Joelle's voice interrupted her.

"Do you have a headache or something?" Joelle asked.

"Huh?"

"You just seem sort of . . . distracted or something."

"Oh. Sorry," Ellie said. "Was thinking about homework. And, I guess, the meet too."

"Yeah. Well, I just hope none of their swimmers are super-fast starters."

"Yeah, I'm not really sure if they are," Ellie murmured, now wondering if they were also fast transitioners. She hooked her pointer finger around her necklace's chain. "But I'll let you know if I can find out!"

Joelle gave her a funny look. "How would you find out?"

Ellie shrugged and zipped her Stingrays jacket all the way up, concealing the silver-and-blue charm.

Joelle left lunch a few minutes early in order to stop at her locker before the next period. Maybe she could get some insight into the nuances of the

Barracuda's starting and transition techniques with her Future Necklace, Ellie figured. She wrapped her fingers around her charm and closed her eyes.

Joelle, rolling her eyes. Her swim cap on, goggles on her forehead, standing on the pool deck, blue and white backstroke flags in the background.

Weird. Joelle wasn't much of an eye roller, to Ellie's knowledge. The vision clearly took place during their upcoming meet—the blue and white flags were Barracuda colors. Someone on the team must have annoyed her. Maybe Hamburger Mike was trying to offer a guerrilla-style nutrition lesson again. That would definitely irritate the heck out of Ellie, so she didn't see why it wouldn't bother her friend too. That must be it. She'd have to remember to warn Joelle that she was in for a lecture about protein sandwiches.

As it turned out, the Barracudas were loud cheerers. Unclear if it was due to their vocals alone or because of some sort of special acoustic nightmare built into the structure of their home pool, but the Stingrays could hear them from the moment they got off the bus and entered the aquatic center. Ellie and Joelle shared a look, both girls adjusting their enormous swim bags on their shoulders.

"Ugh, I wish this were an outdoor situation," Joelle complained as they walked into the visitors' locker room while she was fidgeting with the zipper on her jacket. "The sky is better at absorbing sound because it's so high up. Well, I made that up, but it seems like it could be correct. Roofs are not swimmers' friends."

Ellie nodded.

After changing into her suit and selecting a pair of goggles from her bag, Ellie went to the mirrors over the sinks to tuck in the stray hairs beneath her purple race cap. While her teammates chatted and dressed, familiar thoughts began to pick up pace in her mind.

Will I be able to focus if I have a lane assignment next to the Barracudas' cheering side of the pool? Will the two-hand touch prove impossible this time? Just because I did it once doesn't mean I can do it again under this kind of pressure! Will I win my races? If I lose, will it be totally humiliating or just sort of humiliating?

As Ellie's thoughts threatened to take over, the blue stone on her charm caught her eye in the mirror.

Right. She had her Future Necklace. At least some of those questions could be answered. Before tucking the charm beneath the collar of her suit, she thought to do a quick check to see what was down the line. Ellie closed her eyes.

"Hey!" Joelle chirped, interrupting Ellie for the second time that day.

"Oh, gosh, sorry! Did I do it again? You were visualizing, weren't you? My bad! I didn't want to interrupt, I was just going to wait, but I did that to Zarah the other day when I had a question about the shower and she said lurking and being creepy was just as bad as interrupting. Anyway . . ." Joelle paused, presumably to catch her breath.

"It's okay. I wasn't visualizing. I was just . . ." Ellie's voice trailed off. There really was no good way to explain it. "Preparing."

"Right! Okay, do that. But do you want some lavender oil again?"

"Sure." Ellie ducked her head down. Would she ever get used to being this tall?

"You wear your birthstone necklace during meets?" Joelle asked as she dabbed the oil between Ellie's eyebrows.

"Oh. Yeah," Ellie answered, remembering for the first time in a while that her Future Necklace could masquerade as an astrological piece of jewelry. "It stays tucked under my suit so it doesn't get in the way or anything."

"Cool. Jewelry while swimming would so distract me. I even take my stud earrings out."

"Right," Ellie said, lavender wafting into her nose.

"So, um, also, can you maybe cheer for me at the end of my lane during my breaststroke race? I'm, like, really nervous about that one for some reason. I think that's the race I was swimming when I had my cement dream. And Stargaze mentioned something about me struggling with being stuck today, so . . . yeah. I'm nervous. I checked the heat sheet and it's event number six, right before your butterfly race, so you should have time. But only if it doesn't, um, interrupt you again."

Joelle finished her monologue and smiled up at Ellie without showing her teeth.

"Of course," Ellie told her friend. "I'll be there."

In very non-Mariposa fashion, the meet began right on time. Sort of. The announcer called the first event, the girls' fifty-yard free, right at 4:30 sharp. Ellie had to scramble to get to the block, though once she was there, she found herself waiting. The refs huddled around the PA system, plugging and unplugging wires seemingly at random.

Ellie bounced on her toes to stay warm. After the fifty free, she'd have her backstroke race, a short break, then her butterfly. She'd written all the info from the heat sheet on the back of her hand with her trusty purple Sharpie. She was ready to go. Ellie adjusted her goggles, trying to tune out the exuberant shouts around her, and waited. She'd used her necklace once during warm-ups, but all she saw in the blue-tinted vision was a pool full of thrashing swimmers from a mid-race point of view. Not super helpful. Or something she necessarily needed a Future Necklace to predict. It was a swim meet; of *course* the pool water would be choppy and full of racers once the competition began.

Now, though, the pool before her was calm. Blue and white backstroke flags hung limp across the width. She had a good view of the stands from up there, which were to the right on an upper level looking down at the pool. Her mom was stuck working, so

Ellie wasn't quite sure why she'd glanced over to begin with. A man with a red beard stood at the end of the second row. It was Andy.

Huh. She hadn't realized he was coming. That was . . . nice of him. Part of her was surprised he wasn't wearing that red apron of his.

"Oooooh, I'm heating up!" Snacks shouted from the sideline.

"That's a fever coming on!" Top Five finished, clapping his hands so hard Ellie truly thought he'd break a bone.

"Stingrays, Stingrays, Stingrays!" the Tornado Girls chanted arm in arm.

Ellie stood a little straighter on her block. What was taking so long? It was time to go! The referees appeared to be talking amongst themselves by their table.

She stole a glance at the Barracudas in the neighboring lanes. Both swimmers were a head shorter than her. Ellie returned her attention straight ahead, her lane a calm aqua path. Down at the end, Joelle hopped up and down. Maybe to stay loose, but just as likely because she was too hyped or nervous to stand still.

"You got this, E!" she thought she heard Joelle yell.

Okay. Ellie had another few seconds, right? No sound from the announcer yet; the referees remained in conversation. The anticipation was driving her crazy. Really, what better time to sneak a quick necklace check? Ellie clenched her eyes shut (nobody could see behind her goggles anyway), pretended to scratch an itch under her collarbone, and waited for the vision to arrive.

Blue and white flags before a high white ceiling.

Ellie opened her eyes. Then glanced at the ceiling. Same one from her vision. That was it? Just a flash of her swimming her upcoming backstroke race and nothing more? No, there had to be something more in there, another hint.

"Swimmers, take your marks!"

Along with her competitors, Ellie leaned over, her fingertips grazing her toes. The entire pool hushed. The sudden shift from cacophony to silence felt like whiplash. Why had her Future Necklace shown such a pointless vision? Ellie tried to remember if the image of the flags indicated any movement in the air, an indoor breeze of some sort. Were there any splashes in the periphery? She couldn't recall . . .

BEEP!

The start of the race registered only as Ellie saw the other swimmers' bodies entering the water. She dove off the block with as much force as possible in an effort to make up her lag. Normally, Ellie waited exactly four strokes before taking her first breath, but she couldn't afford that right now. She needed to hustle! Ellie was halfway down the length of the pool before she gulped for air, already half a body length behind the Barracuda in lane three. She had a lot of catching up to do.

But as Ellie neared the wall for a flip turn, she had an idea: Why not use the Future Necklace real quick during her transition underwater? Easy. No problem. It wouldn't disrupt her stoke, no way. Maybe she'd get some helpful, race saving intel just in the nick of time.

So Ellie did. After the flip, right as she jammed her feet against the wall to propel herself forward, instead of shooting her right hand forward to meet her left, she grasped her charm. Immediately, a vision appeared.

Touching the wall, popping her head up, breath-
less. Those in the other lanes with their goggles
off, resting.

Ellie was going to lose this race. She would come in dead last. The Future Necklace proved it. Ellie resumed her stroke but realized she didn't need to kick so hard. No point in going 110 percent if she was going to come in eighth anyway. Might as well save some energy for the races ahead.

So, while it was never fun to lose a race, when Ellie hit her hand against the wall twenty-two yards later, she wasn't surprised that she'd come in last. Sure, the loss stung, but at least her lungs didn't. She'd made the smart choice and conserved energy.

"Shake it off," Brianna and Tye both encouraged her when Ellie got out of the pool. They offered high fives as Ellie moved to the bleachers for water.

"Let's go now!" Coach Puma called, followed with a couple of harsh claps. Ellie saw her coach's eyes trained on the pool. Just as Ellie walked by, she shouted, "Focus!"

Okay, first race down. Not the best start, but that was okay. Ellie only had a short break before her backstroke race. She went to the team bench to regroup. Behind her, swimmers in the next event took their marks. The starting beep went off and once again, the indoor pool nearly combusted with cheers. Facing the wall, Ellie grasped her Future Necklace and closed her eyes. At the top of a quick breath in, the vision appeared.

Blurry aqua water.

And that was it. The vision was more of a static screen saver than an actual event. Ellie tried again, but the Future Necklace only yielded the same result. Weird. She'd try once more before her butterfly race, once her backstroke was over.

"Girls' fifty-yard backstroke!" the announcer called. Whew, this meet sure was moving quickly. Ellie concealed her charm and returned to the starting blocks.

The backstroke race went off without a hitch. Without the pressure of diving off the block (why was starting in the water so much easier?) or worrying about the two-hand touch, the two laps were a breeze. Since Coach Puma had her working on backstroke drills all week, the race didn't feel as unfamiliar as it did against the Dolphins. Not that it was a big deal anyway. Ellie still had her sights on butterfly. At least she'd contributed a second-place finish.

"One race at a time, everyone. One race at a time, let's go!" Coach Puma said, pacing up and down the side of lane one. Her sunglasses, Ellie noticed, were uncharacteristically absent.

Ellie stood behind Top Five and Snacks on the pool deck for the next couple of races, cheering now and then, but mostly she was thinking about the last vision she'd received. Never before had one been so . . . bland? Plain? Unhelpful? It was the bottom of the pool—that was obvious—but so what? Why was that an image the Future Necklace decided she was "ready to receive," or whatever?

The Stingrays placed well in the next couple of races, Hamburger Mike not missing an opportunity to flex his muscles and roar after finishing first place in backstroke and Snacks giving Top Five high fives before she took the block for her next race.

"Let's go!" Ellie shouted, but her mind was elsewhere. Her butterfly race was fast approaching and she was getting more unnerved by the second. She needed her Future Necklace to help, and she needed it stat. Ellie stepped back from the pool deck to find some solace by the bleachers.

"Girls' fifty-yard breaststroke," the announcer called way in the background as Ellie sat down, legs crossed on the bench, facing the pale blue tiled wall.

Ellie kept her eyes shut, hand wrapped around the charm. She took a deep, deep breath, inhaling over the count of five.

Blurry aqua water.

Ellie tried again.

Blurry aqua water.

Ellie tried again. And again. And again. Same vision every time.

Had the Future Necklace gotten too waterlogged or something? Did the pool chemicals or chlorine damage it? The instructions never mentioned anything about that. What was the deal with all the blue? That didn't even make sense. Like, absolutely zero sense.

Bonkers.

Cheering behind her indicated that the last race was over and she was up next. Irritated, she released the charm from her right hand and hurried back out onto the pool deck.

A minute later, Ellie stood atop the block on lane five. She kept her eyes on her toes and tried to take a deep breath. The starting beep blared, and Ellie was off, exploding from the block like popcorn after two minutes and twenty seconds in the microwave.

After a few dolphin kicks underwater, Ellie breeched, throwing both arms forward in unison. Splashes from the lanes on either side indicated she was neck and neck with her competition.

Ellie's mind and body accelerated as she approached the turn. She'd need to remember the front-flip transition technique that proved so solid during time trials. Unfortunately, what she hadn't remembered was to tuck her Future Necklace back into her bathing suit.

Dangly jewelry and athletics did not mix.

Three yards from the wall, Ellie stretched both arms high overhead and arched her back to lever her head out of the water for an enormous final breath before the turn. Right as the air hit her lungs, her chin caught against something. Something thin and metal and—*snap!*

Disoriented, Ellie's stroke hiccuped and then came to a full stop. Through her goggles, Ellie saw her necklace, charm and chain, drifting down toward the bottom of the pool.

So Ellie did what anyone else in the middle of a race whose magic necklace unexpectedly broke as they approached a transition would do. She bobbled. Hesitated. Faltered.

Should I reach down and grab it real quick? It's just right there! It shouldn't slow me down too much, right?!

Though Ellie's stroke was officially on pause, her momentum from the nearly full lap before continued to carry her forward. Forward to the wall. Forward still, while Ellie's attention remained on the drifting necklace, debating if she should get it. Instinctively, Ellie put out her left hand to touch the wall to prepare to push off in the other direction.

A one-hand touch.

Quickly, Ellie rushed her right hand to tap the wall as well, spinning around for the second lap ahead of her. It was too late. Both her necklace and the competing butterflyers were beyond her reach.

Ellie finally finished the race. Dead last. Five seconds behind the seventh-place finisher. But the time didn't matter one bit. In the most unpredictable and, frankly, epic fashion, Ellie had flubbed the two-hand touch. She was disqualified.

Ellie kept her eyes on the ground as she pulled herself out of the water. She didn't look up to see if her teammates offered her any conciliatory high fives and heard not a single "shake it off." That wasn't even her primary concern, anyway. Ellie needed to get back to the far end of lane seven to see where her broken necklace had landed. Once she'd done that, she'd have to find a way to dive in and retrieve it. ASAP.

Before Ellie could get halfway down the length of the pool, she ran into Joelle. Literally, ran into her. Her short but mighty teammate stood in her path right at the pole holding up the backstroke flag.

"Um, sorry. I was just trying to get something." Then, seeing that her friend wasn't moving, Ellie spilled her guts. "Did you see that? Worst race ever! I'm never going to get on the IM relay team, like, ever, I'll probably be fired from butterfly, and my necklace fell off in the middle of the pool and what if I can't get it back?"

Joelle looked at her right in the face and rolled her eyes. The picture was familiar. Because she'd seen it before. Her Future Necklace had shown her this very thing, though never would Ellie have imagined that she'd be on the receiving end of Joelle's expression.

"I thought you were going to be at the end of my lane. For my race."

Ellie's stomach dropped. She'd forgotten. Completely forgotten.

"You promised," Joelle peeped, deflating a bit. It looked like she was about to say something else, but a swell of cheers defeated the possibility of Ellie being able to hear whatever that might be. It didn't matter. Joelle brushed past her, joining the rest of their teammates to root on swimmers in the final two events, the girls' and boys' IM relay races.

Was Ellie supposed to chase after Joelle? Well, not chase—no running on the pool deck. But go after? Apologize? Of course, she'd messed up, she knew that. She just needed to find her necklace first. Then, perhaps, the magic jewelry could help her predict how to correct her error.

"Boys' IM relay!" the announcer called.

Ellie scuffled to the end of lane five. She needed to get there before the race began. Even if it was temporarily out of reach, just laying eyes on her Future Necklace might make Ellie feel better.

"Swimmers, take your marks!"

Ellie arrived at the water's edge, the pool's surface nearly placid, calmed since the last race. She leaned over the water, nudging Brianna and an eighth grader aside to get a better view.

When she looked down toward the bottom of the pool, right where her Future Necklace snapped off her neck only minutes earlier, all she saw was blurry aqua water.

The necklace was nowhere in her field of vision.

Chapter twelve

Despite Ellie's horrific personal performance, the Stingrays beat the Barracudas. They were 2–0 to start the season. Mrs. James invited everyone back to Pies Only to celebrate once again, but Ellie wasn't in the mood. Not for pie, not for Joelle or Coach Puma, not even to face her teammates. She claimed "old swimmer's knee," something she made up on the spot, as an excuse to leave.

So Andy brought her home. Good thing he showed up to watch the meet after all. On the car ride back to her apartment, some weird music with a violin and no words played in the background. Eventually, he asked if he could turn on the soccer game. Something about stoppage time. Ellie didn't know why anyone would want to *listen* to a soccer game, but she told him to go for it. She wasn't paying attention, anyway.

Her Future Necklace was gone.

Well, it was probably somewhere. Ellie hadn't been able to find it, though. She had hoped that after the meet was over, she'd be able to spot it at the bottom of the pool. Maybe once the commotion in the water died down it would be there in a corner, adrift but waiting for her. No luck. The Future Necklace was nowhere in sight. She'd wanted to ask Coach Puma if there was someone she could contact about it, but after her completely bonkers performance, Ellie was afraid to ask for any favors.

"Tough loss." Andy sighed, switching off the satellite radio as they turned into the Inman Terrace Apartments parking lot.

Ellie wasn't sure if he was talking about the soccer game or her races.

"For what it's worth," Andy continued, shifting the car into park, "your team seems to have a great vibe going on. You all really know how to cheer."

Ellie nodded and unclipped her seat belt.

"Quite the squad of stingrays."

"It's fever," Ellie murmured.

"What's that?" Andy asked.

"Nothing."

Ellie's stomach grumbled. The two got out of the car and started up the pathway toward the apartment.

"I sense that you might be disappointed by how things turned out today, but I promise you'll have many amazing races to come."

"How do you know?" Ellie's question came out a little ruder than she intended.

"Well, because I'm a visionary when it comes to sporting outcomes." Andy held open the gate leading to her unit for Ellie to step through. "I'm kidding."

"I know," Ellie replied, though the idea that Andy had a Future Necklace of his own did cross her mind for the quickest of seconds.

"Right," Andy said. "But in all seriousness, I can see how much you care about swimming. Today may have felt off, but you know what you're doing. And you have a great team behind you. It will all come together. Maybe when you least expect it, but it will. One tough performance won't define you as a swimmer."

"Okay, thanks," Ellie whispered.

"That might sound cheesy. But not as cheesy as my lasagna. Which I'm happy to make for you and your mom anytime."

Ellie cracked a smile.

"Okay, thanks," Ellie repeated, this time really meaning it.

She knew Andy was probably right. And he was trying to be nice. He *was* being nice. Why, then, did Ellie still feel so unsettled, as if there were a sharp but invisible splinter deep in her heel, nagging and sharp?

Ellie didn't hear from Joelle all night. No text, no call, no telepathic message, nothing. At first Ellie tried to tell herself it was no big deal. Maybe Joelle was busy with family stuff or doing something with Zarah. Maybe their confrontation wasn't a fight, just a misunderstanding. But the more Ellie obsessed about it, the more uncertain the future of their friendship seemed. Would Joelle forgive her? Might she under-stand that Ellie was just trying to prepare for the meet herself, and she'd made a mistake, but it wasn't intentional? Could Joelle understand what it felt like to be so tall but still feel so small, that she'd found a magic necklace and her attention had been divided ever since?

Ellie wasn't sure if she could. Or if she should. Ellie couldn't blame Joelle for being mad. Truthfully, she probably would be too.

Though Ellie spent countless hours over the weekend imagining every possible answer and outcome to what might become of her and Joelle, she truly had no idea which (if any) prediction would prove true. She wished, more than anything, she had her Future Necklace to show her how things would turn out—if they'd make up and be friends again or if it was all over, so soon after their fun began. By the time Ellie fell asleep Sunday evening, after a long boring weekend filled with *Fanplex Blues* reruns while her mom tried to sell houses to strangers, Ellie feared she'd lost more than just a magic necklace.

Chapter Thirteen

So, Ellie began her Future Necklace–free life. Okay, restarted. She'd only had the necklace for a couple of weeks, but already it felt like a lifetime. Without it, she felt as if she'd grown four inches overnight. Again.

No way to know what was coming, Ellie was in the same boat as her teammates on Monday when Coach Puma announced that they'd be doing a dryland. Dryland: a training session focused on strength and conditioning that involved no actual swimming whatsoever and also Ellie's least favorite kind of practice, because if she wanted to stay on land, she would have just picked a sport like track or basketball or even badminton, whatever that entailed. After a rotten weekend, and still no word from Joelle, the last thing Ellie wanted was an awkward practice that didn't involve any swimming.

During stretches, Ellie kept to herself, easily

settling into her old spot on the corner of the mats nearest to the bleachers. She listened to her teammates chat, didn't say anything, and did her best not to worry about how much of the practice ahead would consist of horrible transitions where she didn't know what to do or say or be. The absence of her Future Necklace was so noticeable it was almost loud, because of both her lack of foresight and the way the spot where the charm once landed against her skin burned hot like the August sun.

"It's going to be for animals, I'm thinking," Snacks explained, referencing her astrology app in progress. She chewed a bite-sized candy and stretched her shoulder. "That niche market is way less saturated."

"Dude, I don't know," Top Five chimed in. "Animals are complicated. Do people even want that?"

"OMG, my cat is such a Pisces," Ellie heard Joelle exclaim. Ellie averted her eyes, training her vision on her kneecaps as she leaned over her extended legs for a hamstring stretch. Joelle had never mentioned that she had a cat.

"See?!" Snacks continued. "Stargaze is so relevant for person-to-person chemistry and general vibe information, but it's not enough! Pets are people too!"

Coach Puma approached the stretch mats, interrupting the debate.

"We're going to shake it up today." She wore black leggings and a white racerback tank top. A departure from her usual track pants and very coach-y Mariposa Stingrays pullover. Without wasting any time, Coach Puma instructed, "Yoga day. Everyone spread out on the mats and lie on your backs, arms by your sides, legs out."

Ellie had never done yoga. All those moves looked so . . . twisty. She wasn't sure her way-too-tall body could move in all those directions without falling right over. Plus, she didn't know the names of any of the poses. How would she manage to follow along?

Once Coach Puma started the session, though, Ellie didn't have time to think about any of that. Seemingly one of the few yoga newbies on the team, she had no idea what pose or position or move or whatever they were called came next. The single and last time she'd zoned out, she ended up standing on one leg while everyone else was in a downward-facing dog (okay, she knew the name of that one). Ellie didn't have time to think or even worry about what was coming next, if she was flexible enough, or if she'd manage to balance. Coach Puma's steady flow forced her body and attention to remain nowhere else but in the present.

At the end of the hour, Ellie dripped sweat. She had no idea yoga could be so extreme. By the looks on her teammates' faces, she suspected she wasn't alone in that assessment.

"All right, now that everyone is wiped out, listen up," Coach Puma began. Her timing was spot on. Not even Snacks made a sound, to unwrap a package of cookies or otherwise. At least from Ellie's view, Coach Puma seemed relaxed, calm, and devoid of a single molecule of sweat, despite having led the team through the rigorous sequence herself. "Riptides on Saturday. I know this meet has been on everyone's mind."

Coach Puma was right about that. Ellie's collar-bone burned and her stomach flipped.

"It's true; this will probably be the toughest meet of the season. We aren't going to swim our best, though, if we put too much attention on what's to come. We need to attend to what's right in front of us. And that is busting our butts in practice this week. Disciplined transitions and technique. Supporting one another. Let's focus on what we can control."

"Like looking dooooope in our new jackets!" Top Five called. His comment was rewarded by laughs and even a tooth-filled smile from Coach Puma.

"That too," Coach Puma acquiesced. "Great yoga session today. Thanks to everyone for giving it a shot. Can someone help with rolling in the lane lines? They're using the pool for a trial water aerobics class all evenings this week."

"On it," Snacks declared, jumping to her feet.

"I'll help," Joelle volunteered.

Ellie pressed her fingertips against the dip in her collarbone. If she'd had her Future Necklace, maybe she'd have seen that Joelle would volunteer and then she'd known to jump on the opportunity too. They still hadn't spoken, much less made eye contact, since the meet. Ellie wasn't quite sure how to initiate, well, anything.

Ellie saw Coach Puma was still on the bleachers finishing up a chat with Tye and Brianna. She seized the opening.

"Excuse me, Coach?"

"Yes, El?"

"So I lost something in the pool at the Barracuda

meet." Ellie halted. She shouldn't have been wearing jewelry during competition. Though it wasn't technically a rule, removing jewelry before meets was common practice. She'd known that all along. How could she admit she'd lost her necklace if she shouldn't have had one on her in the first place? Without knowing how Coach Puma might react, but without the benefit of a future-telling device, Ellie had no choice but to choose her words on the fly. "I have—had—this special, um, birthstone necklace, and I think it fell in the pool, but I didn't see it after the meet. I'm not sure if you're friends with the Barracudas' coach or whatever, but is there any way to ask if it got stuck in the pool filters?"

Coach Puma looked at Ellie for a beat before answering. She was a few inches taller. Ellie came up to her chin.

"I'll call over and see," she answered simply.

"Okay, thanks," Ellie peeped. Then, without knowing exactly why or what came over her, she asked, "When did you stop growing? How old were you, I mean? Like, for height."

Ellie couldn't be certain, but she thought she saw Coach Puma's expression soften.

"Oh boy. Let me think," Coach Puma said. Ellie shifted her weight between her feet. "I had a big spurt after eighth grade. And I thought I was done." Ellie exhaled. "But then I had another right before my sophomore year of high school. That caught me by surprise."

"Oh," Ellie replied glumly. Out of the corner of her eye, she saw Snacks and Joelle chatting in rapid fire while they tugged on a lane line together. She couldn't hear what they were saying.

"Everyone is different, though. The extra inches took some getting used to, but eventually I did. It was a big change at first, but soon I hardly even noticed."

Ellie thought about what Coach Puma said all the way home.

When Ellie walked through the front door, she realized the apartment smelled, well, amazing. Which was in no way surprising since Ellie's mom had texted her that Andy was making dinner again. She was starting to expect it.

"Hey, Ellie," Andy called from the kitchen. "Your mom's stuck late at work, but food's in the works."

Ellie stepped into the kitchen and saw Andy's

laptop open on the counter. A soccer game played on the screen while he stood rolling small meatball-looking things between his hands and placing them onto a cookie tray that Ellie didn't realize they owned.

"What are those?" Ellie blurted.

"Sliders!" he said, then, based on Ellie's confused look, added, "tiny hamburgers."

"Cool." To be polite, Ellie inquired, "What smells so good?"

"That would be my famous garlic butter for the fries." He nodded toward a small pot on the stove. She didn't know they had one so tiny. Maybe Andy had brought it.

"We should probably get that soup pot you were talking about, huh?" Ellie offered.

"When the time comes," Andy said with a smile, before returning his attention to the game.

Ellie let her swim bag drop to the floor. She should go unpack—open the pockets, take out her wet bathing suit, the whole drill. Maybe it was the smell of the butter and the garlic, or her curiosity that Andy seemed very invested in soccer (he didn't seem like the sporty type), but Ellie just didn't have it in her.

A whistle sounded from the soccer game, followed

by the roar of the spectators. Andy shouted, "Are you kidding me? He was onsides by a mile!"

Ellie walked around to get a full view of the screen. They watched together. Just from looking, Ellie couldn't quite anticipate what qualified as exciting or tense on her own, but Andy's reactions clued her right in. After a couple of minutes, the ball rolled out of bounds, and a player in a blue jersey picked it up to throw it back in.

"Watch this," Andy advised. "He's been showing off with his throw-ins all game."

Sure enough, with the ball in his hands, the player took a running start and right before crossing over the sideline flipped forward in a handspring, launching the ball halfway down the field. The momentum from the flip must have helped catapult the ball . . .

"I know how to do that!" Ellie exclaimed.

"You do?" Andy asked. "I didn't know you played soccer too."

"Oh no, no way. Land sports aren't my thing," Ellie corrected him. "A flip!" Without thinking, she blurted, "Off the diving board. I just learned this special technique. Want me to teach you?"

Ellie never would have guessed that Andy, her cooking-obsessed soon-to-be stepdad, would be so eager to drop dinner preparations in order to learn a new diving board trick.

"You have to really pretend you're throwing the ball in right when you jump," Ellie explained from the diving board before demonstrating for the fifth time. Her flips were really getting good.

Andy stepped onto the diving board, leaving his glasses on the concrete below. She hoped he wasn't too blind.

"Here goes," he called.

Ellie held her breath. She had a feeling this wasn't going to be a full 360-degree situation.

Andy trotted to the end of the board. He bounced. And bounced again. Then he sort of brought his hands over his head and then flung himself off, rotating 90 degrees, then 180. Was he going to get all the way around, one full rotation? It was gonna be close . . .

Nope.

Andy landed, the water smacking against his lower back.

"Ouuuuch. You okay?" Ellie asked, trying not to giggle when he surfaced.

He grimaced but gave her a thumbs-up.

Ellie sensed he needed a break.

"You're really into watching soccer," Ellie stated once Andy had retrieved his glasses and paddled his way to the shallow end.

"Yeah, I got really into the whole fantasy thing a few years ago. I like to watch, but mostly I like to play."

"I get that."

"Playing soccer, or any sport, really, helps me turn my mind off. You never know what's going to happen before it does—that's sort of the cool thing about sports, I think—they force you to make split decisions and stay in the present. You don't have time to think, but you can train your body to know what to do on instinct."

"Hmm." Ellie sort of got that but sort of didn't. She'd certainly done her fair share of thinking mid-lap, but in her best races, the ones where she felt most at home in the pool, her body really had done the thinking for her. "Do you ever wish you could see the future?"

"Sometimes," Andy answered.

"Like when you asked my mom to marry you?" Ellie hadn't planned on asking him that, but now that she had, she was very curious about the answer.

"Well, no."

"Oh," Ellie replied. "Never mind, then."

"I was very nervous to tell you," Andy admitted. "About the engagement. Part of me wanted to know how that would go in advance."

For the first time, Ellie realized that maybe joining their family was as big a deal for Andy as it was for her. Different, but still a big deal.

Andy was easy to talk to, as it turned out. They chatted about the many differences between soccer and swimming, debated the ethics of zoos, and Ellie even told him a thing or two about astrology, parroting back what she'd absorbed from Snacks. Her Future Necklace had shown her Andy was into cooking, but that was pretty much it. Maybe, Ellie realized, Andy wasn't someone she'd previously been ready to receive.

"Hey, Prunies!" Ellie's mom called from the balcony. "What ya doing down there?"

"Front flipping," Ellie replied.

"Ellie taught me! I almost have it," Andy shouted back.

"Mmm, I wouldn't say *almost*," Ellie teased. "Not a full three-sixty degrees."

"Three-twenty-five?"

"Sure," Ellie agreed. "That's more accurate."

"Speaking of degrees, those oven bake fries might be sort of oven burnt by now," Andy remembered, though he didn't seem bothered by the prospect.

That gave Ellie an idea. An amazing idea, if she did say so herself. So amazing, she wasn't going to take no for an answer.

"So on our swim team, everyone eventually gets a nickname," Ellie explained as they got out of the pool and dried off. "I mean, I don't have one yet, but hopefully I will. It's sort of like the name chooses you."

"My soccer buds call me Pantry."

"I sort of get that." Ellie laughed. "Anyway, I just figured out yours. Like, for us."

"Flip time's over!" Ellie's mom called, impatient. "Dinner's ready!"

Ellie and Andy shared a skeptical look. Maura Greene? Cooking dinner? That didn't sound right.

And it wasn't.

"I thought they were meatballs!" Ellie's mom cried when they walked into the kitchen. A colander full of spaghetti was steaming in the sink and an open can of tomatoes sat on the counter. The fries, along with the sliders, which Ellie's mom had popped in the oven to cook, weren't too burned, at least, though Ellie did think she saw a splatter of tomato sauce on the wall. Maybe the ceiling too.

"Sliders," Ellie and Andy, aka 325, corrected her together.

"Those are in the meatball family!"

"Well, you know, if I was making meatballs, it would be a completely different flavor profile. I mean, you don't even use the same spices . . ."

Now it was Ellie and her mom's turn to share a laugh.

"Okay, okay, I'm being nerdy about it. But it's true." Andy didn't waste any time getting back into his apron. "Okay, let's improvise here."

So they all finished making dinner together. Ellie's mom stirred the garlic butter into the pasta; Ellie spooned tomato sauce onto the sliders while Andy sliced cheese. They snacked on crispy oven fries as an appetizer.

"This is unlike anything I've ever made," Andy said, scratching his head as they waited for the cheese to melt on top of the saucy sliders.

"It's gonna be good," Ellie and her mom said in unison.

And it was.

Standing around the kitchen island, Ellie, her mom, and 325 devoured bowls of tomato slider noodles. Ellie couldn't see into the future, of course, but she sensed that this wouldn't be the last time the three of them would share a bizarre and delicious meal while standing together in the kitchen.

Chapter Fourteen

Practices leading up to the Riptide meet were different. Not so much the drills. Even without a Future Necklace, Ellie was starting to get the hang of Coach Puma's rotations. The fever vibe, though. That was different. Everyone was either super focused or super nervous. Transition time between drills didn't feel so extensive, though Ellie had offered Snacks feedback on the beta version of her app while doing a few kickboard laps side by side, so maybe that accounted for some of it. As a non-pet-owner, Snacks said Ellie's opinion was still just as valuable for purposes of devil's advocacy.

At first Ellie didn't want to admit it to herself, but without spending so much time using her Future Necklace, trying to interpret her visions or wondering if her necklace would show the glimpse she hoped for in that particular moment, she felt at ease in a way that was both familiar and new.

By the end of the week, Ellie realized that her Future Necklace had solved some problems, true, but it had also created quite a few. Sure, she didn't know in advance that her mom would try her hand at cooking dinner on her own Tuesday night, resulting in completely inedible chicken that Ellie dutifully choked down, but really, after the slider attempt, she sensed more Maura Greene home-cooking attempts were inevitable. Ellie had had a pop quiz in geometry, but she'd stayed on top of her homework every night and found it easier to pay attention in class these days, so she'd aced it.

She tried to keep in mind what 325 said about sports and staying in the moment, and she had to admit, he was sort of right. Transitions, both of the two-hand touch variety and between-drill-water-break variety, hadn't thrown her off. She just took them as they came instead of worrying. And when Ellie wasn't worrying so much, turned out she didn't zone out as much either. In second grade, Ellie had a teacher who went on and on about how moles have extremely good senses of smell to compensate for their lack of sight. Ellie sort of felt like that. Without her Future Necklace—her sixth sense, in a way—her listening and general attention to what was going on right in front of her was suddenly heightened. She wasn't the only one who seemed to notice.

"Great work this week," Coach Puma said at the end of practice on Friday. The Riptides meet was the next morning, so the session had been pretty mellow with lots of time for cooldown and stretching. Ellie had spent some time on the mat suggesting new top five categories for Top Five and even engaged with Hamburger Mike in a heated debate about the merits of sliders. Joelle sat near the Tornado Girls, but Ellie wasn't sure if she was *with* with them or just sitting sort of close by.

"Thanks!" Ellie replied. And then, because it seemed like the right time, not because she'd planned it, she admitted, "I've had a hard time with, um, transitions. In general. I know my two-hand touch has been . . . bonkers. But I'm going to keep working on it, and if there's ever room for me on the IM relay team, I'd really like to swim that race one day."

Coach Puma nodded and maybe even smiled. "That's good to hear. You've been incredibly focused this week. Present. In a way I haven't seen you all season."

Ellie thought to ask Coach Puma if she'd gotten any word about her necklace, but the impulse passed. She didn't want to ruin the moment. It wasn't every day she got a multi-sentence compliment from her swim coach. Ellie wanted to luxuriate in the feeling.

Coach Puma gave her shoulder a squeeze and blew her whistle.

"Let's wrap it up, everyone. Quick cleanup, then back on the bus for team dinner. Who's got lane lines?"

"On it," Joelle and Snacks announced at the same time.

"Kickboards?" Coach Puma called.

Without a moment's hesitation, Ellie replied, "Got it!"

"Tyanna, you both can get flippers and pull buoys."

Just like cleanup at the end of practice, there were multiple elements to a swim meet. After a tough but fun week of practices, Ellie understood that more than ever. Kickboards and relay races were just two parts of a much larger fever.

The Stingrays went straight from practice to Pies Only for the team dinner. Snacks and Top Five organized the entire production. Since the Riptides meet was on a Saturday morning, they determined that in lieu of a fashion-related team spirit pump-up situation, an in-person group activity was the next best (or maybe even better) option.

Top Five's mom sectioned off the entire back area of the shop for the fever. Boxes of pizza awaited them on the long yellow tables when they arrived.

"Pizza *pies*," Mrs. James emphasized, welcoming the team inside.

Ellie had planned to apologize to Joelle at the team dinner. She'd envisioned getting a seat next to her as a way to break the ice. Then, if they needed, they could step outside and chat over a slice of pecan, perhaps. But somehow, amid the chaos of fifteen middle schoolers swarming a restaurant and claiming spots at the table, Ellie got smooshed between Hamburger Mike and the Tornado Girls. Joelle landed in a chair on the opposite end.

Okay, Ellie thought. *No big deal.* Easy enough to regroup. She'd just find her on their way out. Maybe that would be better anyway. They'd be fed and thinking clearly. On the bright side, Ellie could practice her speech in her head a few more times.

I'm so sorry, Joelle, she'd start. *I was a bad friend and I'll never do it again. Please forgive me.*

Hopefully, Joelle would and they'd live happily ever after as friends and everything would be fine . . . right? For the first time ever, Ellie dared not let her mind consider a less desirable alternative.

Between pizza pie courses and pie-pie courses, Ellie excused herself to the restroom. Not because she had to go, but because Hamburger Mike's monologue was simply relentless. She was pleased to discover that the bathroom was also entirely yellow.

Ellie stood at the sink and stared at herself in the mirror. The counter came up to her hip bones, a bit higher than the ones in the Mariposa locker rooms, lower than the one at home. She took out her hair tie to redo her ponytail, noticing her arm muscles under her T-shirt. She appeared a little stronger than she remembered. Too bad her necklace was lost. Regardless of its powers, she liked the way it looked for fashion purposes. The aqua stone really popped against the purple on the team jackets, which had become a wardrobe staple.

Ellie began to twist her hair into a clean topknot when the door to the bathroom opened. In the mirror, Ellie saw Joelle walk in. Completely caught off guard, Ellie fully froze. This wasn't how she'd imagined them meeting. Not at all.

"Oh, hi."

"Hi," Ellie responded, her hair still mid-updo, still looking at Joelle in the mirror. "Don't worry, I washed my hands."

"Don't worry, I'm not even here to use the bathroom. I just needed a break." The girls stood, silent, assessing each other's reflections in the mirror for a moment.

"You're not wearing your birthstone necklace," Joelle observed.

"It broke," Ellie muttered. The top of her chest burned.

Joelle shuffled her feet and tapped her fingers against her leg. "Okay, I can go. Sorry to interrupt if you were fixing your hair or visualizing or something."

Joelle turned to walk out the door. Suddenly, Ellie felt like she was approaching a transition—a flip turn or two-hand touch—but sort of the real-life version. Transitions were never best executed by overthinking. Ellie knew that from personal experience. Sometimes you just had to rely on your technique, or, in this case, your heart.

"Wait!" Ellie called, her voice echoing off the bathroom tiles. The acoustics, similar to an indoor pool, were oddly comforting. "I want to say something important."

Joelle turned and spoke before Ellie could continue. "It really hurt my feelings that you forgot about my race, but I didn't think we'd have to stop being friends because of it. I really want to be friends!"

"OMG, me too! I so want to be friends, but I wasn't sure if this fight meant we weren't. I hope that's not true."

"And maybe it was silly, and maybe I shouldn't admit it because it's weird or something, and Zarah says I should consider being less weird, but I hoped that we could ride to meets together for pump-up purposes and you'd maybe sleep over at some point, and then you could verify that maybe Zarah is the weird one, and there's this show I like—"

"There's this show *I* like! And I think you'll love it too, but if you don't that's also okay, and—"

Suddenly, the toilet flushed. Ellie and Joelle's exchange came to a halt. A woman with a monochrome-yellow outfit, but who definitely did not work there, came out of the stall.

"FYI, you both are yelling!" she shouted, before washing her hands and leaving. Joelle and Ellie didn't move a muscle until they heard the door shut behind her. At which point they started laughing so hard, tears flowed down their cheeks like an open faucet.

"Did you—"

"No, I—"

"Her outfit—"

"Can you—"

More giggles. And more. And more. They laughed until they were out of breath, which was actually quite a feat for two athletes with such cardiovascular strength.

Once they calmed down, Ellie began again. Not with the exact apology that she'd planned in her head but based on what felt true that very moment.

"Joelle, for real. I'm really sorry I blew off your race. I was in this zone where I thought I needed to prepare a certain way and try to figure out the future before it happened, but I realized that's not a way to be a swimmer or a friend or even live, really. I won't do it again."

Joelle smiled, and without saying anything, Ellie knew that everything between them was okay. Maybe not forever—friends got in fights sometimes, apparently—but they could cross that bridge when they got there. For now, they were okay.

Ellie hadn't checked Stargaze in a while, not since Joelle mentioned she'd friended her on it after the Dolphins meet. That night before bed, instead of rewatching old Olympic swim victories that she'd seen a million times, Ellie thought to read her horoscope. It wasn't a Future Necklace, but maybe the stars had some interesting insight. Ellie opened the app.

Pay attention, my dear Pisces. Life is conspiring to show you new ways of living and understanding things. But if you don't pause and take time to appreciate what is already in front of you, you may just miss them. Stop sitting around worrying about tomorrow when today is a gift you have yet to open.

Ellie remembered what Joelle had once said about astrology. How it wasn't a way to predict the future, but rather a fun guide for how to think about yourself and your life.

Hmm . . .

Maybe she'd been taking the Future Necklace way too literally. Sure, it actually showed her snippets from the future. But maybe what those snippets were really meant to do was call her attention to the present.

Had her Future Necklace really shown anything she couldn't have put together had she not just been paying better attention? Okay, sure, she might never have known about some of the school assignments or the kick set. But the bigger things. Joelle coming over to hang out. They'd been talking about doing something after school all week. Ellie could have reasonably anticipated an at-home hang. And even with Andy! Ellie's mom talked about him all the time, which was not something she did with other boyfriends. They'd been on vacation together. It wasn't really all that out of the blue that they decided to get married.

And then the swimming. At first the Future Necklace had been great, but in the end, Ellie had let it take over, just another preoccupation sucking her attention away from her strokes.

The Future Necklace spelled it out: Ellie had only

seen what she was ready to receive. The necklace tried to warn her about Joelle, to pay attention to her behavior in the moment. What if the Future Necklace was really a tool for which to remain in the present? Now that Ellie had no necklace, no way to see glimpses of the future whatsoever, worrying about it suddenly seemed like such a waste of time.

The present is all we've got, Ellie thought as she slowly drifted to sleep.

Chapter Fifteen

There was so much Ellie couldn't predict. There always would be. But there was also a lot she could at least anticipate. Enough that, if done consistently, it might help the unknowns feel slightly less scary.

Routines. Ellie decided to focus on those. Some old, some changing, some new.

Ellie woke up early on this meet day, no snoozing. Saturday meets were a little different, not just because they were in the morning but because everyone arrived on their own, not together via school bus. In no way did Joelle live en route to the Mariposa pool, but after Ellie explained that it was really important that the girls arrive together to go over their races and have some general "swim talk" beforehand, her mom was happy to scoop up Ellie's friend.

"I made a playlist," Joelle announced as she climbed into the back seat. "It's basically a Hat Girls slash Boys Jump! tribute, but it's very good for the pump-up."

Ellie's mom plugged Joelle's phone into the car stereo, and the three of them sang all the way to the pool. Rarely did all three know the same lyric to any song, but at no point in the twenty-minute, windows-down ride was there a moment of silence.

When the girls arrived at the Mariposa pool, ponytails dancing against the backs of their fever jackets, they went straight to the locker room. Ellie changed, retrieved her meet goggles and cap from her bag, and went to the mirrors to tuck in the strays. Joelle approached with her vial of lavender oil. Ellie lowered her head and Joelle dabbed the scent onto her third eye.

"Actually, this is maybe weird, but can you put some right here below the little U between my collar-bones?" Ellie asked, touching the spot, which felt more flushed by the second. Joelle did.

Maybe it was the smell, or maybe the oil really did ease her flush, but after a slow inhale over the count of three, Ellie felt calmer throughout every inch of her body. Even in the extra four that were starting to feel not-so-extra.

Once on the pool deck, they dropped their equally enormous swim bags by the Stingrays' bench and went to check the heat sheet taped to the wall. Ellie scanned the busy document for her usual races.

"OMG!" Joelle squealed. "Look!"

Ellie's eyes found Joelle's finger on the page. At first, she couldn't believe it.

#1 (Girls IM Relay)
MSR
Greene, Ellie (back)
Wheatley, Brianna (fly)
Pike, Joelle (breast)
Choi, Sophie (free)

There they were. Ellie Green and Joelle Pike. Contributing backstroker and breaststroker on the girls' IM relay team.

"No way!" Ellie shouted, blinking to make sure the information was real.

It was.

Of *course* Coach Puma had slotted her in at back-stroke. Duh, duh, duh. Suddenly, she felt so silly. Why had her heart been so set on butterfly all this time? Sure, she'd dropped time over the last week, but she'd been breaking records, personal and otherwise, in backstroke since the Dolphin meet. This whole time Ellie had been setting all her hopes on the chance to swim fly, when really the truth was obvious: Her backstroke was fierce. The transition to backstroke swimmer certainly wasn't something she'd have seen coming before the start of the season, but now after a couple of meets, the race was starting to feel just right.

"Front flip fever," Ellie and Joelle cheered as they embraced, as teammates and as friends.

The Stingray fans came to cheer, no doubt about that. Halfway through warm-ups, the stands were completely full and buzzing.

Joelle pointed out her dad, stepmom, and Zarah, who was definitely as cool and maybe as scary as Ellie had expected. Ellie's mom and 325 brought signs, which would have been beyond embarrassing if 325's illustrations of a fever of stingrays zipping past a school of fish wasn't so darn eye-catching. Cooking, soccer, and now an artist? Jeez. She felt like she was learning something new about the guy every day.

"El, before I forget," Coach Puma said as Ellie stopped at the bench to get a sip of water at the end of her warm-up. "Here's the necklace you asked about. The Barracudas' coach found it earlier this week, but I kept forgetting to bring it to practice."

Out of her pocket, Coach Puma retrieved a key-shaped charm with an aquamarine stone on a silver chain. She placed it in Ellie's open hand.

"Excited to see you in the medley today." Coach Puma smiled, and they high-fived. "Go get 'em."

Ellie was stunned. She stood in the middle of the pool deck and stared at the necklace in the palm of her hand. The necklace stared right back, the gem as radiant as ever. But the chain was broken; there would be no way to clasp it around her neck before getting it properly fixed. Still, there was no reason it shouldn't work.

Like putting on an old practice suit, perfectly stretchy and familiar, unknowns that the Future Necklace might clarify rushed to Ellie's head.

Will the Riptides start the relay fast or wait until the

third leg to turn on the jets? Will my teammates be disappointed in me if I don't lead off the relay strong? Is this my first and only chance to ever compete in the IM relay?

Before Ellie's spiraling thoughts could pick up the pace, Snacks's booming voice cut through the air. "This temperature is rising, baby!" she called, strutting across the pool deck, pretending to fan her face.

"Oooh weee, I'm heating up!" Top Five added, doing the same. They really were quite the duo.

Ellie peered down at the charm. All she had to do was close her hand and eyes. It was that simple. Or was it?

"I feel a fever coming on!" the co-captains shouted together.

Why did Ellie need to see a glimpse of the meet ahead, anyway? She was going to swim her hardest no matter what. She'd cheer on her teammates every second she wasn't in the water. She'd probably get a little nervous as she approached the block, but she didn't think there was much she could do about that, even if she could confirm it. A pool is just a hole in the ground with water in it.

"Ninety-nine point nine degrees!" Snacks declared.

"One hundred and two and rising!" Top Five piggybacked.

The Stingrays started to gather on the pool deck around their captains. Ellie stood frozen, caught between the bench and her team.

"Stingray!" Snacks called, cupping her hands around her mouth for maximum effect.

"Fever!" Top Five answered, somehow matching Snacks's volume.

One by one, Ellie let her questions and concerns slip away. Just like her practice suits from last season, and just like most of her pants, she'd outgrown them.

"Say it with us now!" they called together.

Ellie smiled at her necklace, held the charm against that not-so-burning spot below the dip in her collarbone, then stashed it in the outer pocket of her swim bag, along with her Sharpies and rubber-duck key chain with a mystery key to nowhere. Maybe she'd regret not seeing what was to come, but she didn't want to risk missing anything happening right in front of her in order to find out.

"Stingray!" half of Ellie's teammates chanted as Ellie darted to join the pack.

"Fever!" Ellie screamed, throwing her arm around Joelle.

"Stingray!"

"Fever!"

"Stingray!"

"Fever!"

The team continued to chant, naturally drawing into a tight huddle.

"On three!" Snacks shouted.

In unison, Snacks and Top Five yelled, "One . . . two . . . three!"

"GO, STINGRAYS!" Ellie and her teammates cheered at the very top of their lungs.

It was eight minutes past the scheduled start time.

"Event number one, girls' IM relay!" the announcer finally called.

"Let's go!" Coach Puma called. "Swimmers to the blocks!"

Ellie took one last glimpse at her swim bag, knowing full well what rested in the outside zipper pocket. Without thinking or worrying a moment more, high-fiving her teammates all along the way, she marched over to lane three to swim her race.

If Ellie had used her Future Necklace that morning, she might have seen that the Stingrays would beat the Riptides for the first time in years. She might have received a flash vision of herself cheering at the end of lane three, shouting "Front flip fever!" right as Joelle transitioned into her second lap. She might have seen the group celebration once the victors were announced, a mess of hugs, cheers, and even tears, though no picture could accurately convey the elation of the moment.

If Ellie continued to use the Future Necklace over the course of the season, she could have seen snippet after snippet of her and Joelle learning increasingly advanced diving board tricks and making pump-up playlists late into the night during sleepovers. More likely than not, Ellie would have caught an early glimpse of a totally disorganized kitchen full of half-unpacked boxes and more kitchen equipment than one person, or even three, could possibly need. She probably would have seen a flash of her debating about the best drawer for cutlery with her soon-to-be stepfather, and realizing he might be right about the forks, but definitely not about soup pot storage placement. She'd likely have advance knowledge of the shiny trophy the Mariposa Stingrays would receive when they placed first in the end-of-season invitational, and the numerous medals she'd earn, mostly in backstroke, but some in butterfly and free too. But none of those visions could have communicated that by the end of the swim season, Ellie would feel like she'd been five foot six inches tall her entire life.

And if Ellie had kept on using her Future Necklace over the summer, she'd certainly have seen that the wedding in Mexico would be beautiful, and snorkeling the second time would be even cooler than the first. She'd probably learn ahead of time that at the beginning of eighth grade, Coach Puma would name her and Joelle—aka Front and Flip—co-captains of the Stingrays, though the feeling of pride that came with welcoming a slew of newbies into the fever alongside her best friend would still be a surprise.

But Ellie didn't continue to use her Future

Necklace, so she didn't see any of that. Once Ellie tucked her Future Necklace into the outside pocket of her swim bag, that's where it remained. No, Ellie Greene didn't see any more blue hour–tinted visions of her future, instead letting the present unfold one surprising, unpredictable, and exciting moment at a time.

Acknowledgments

I am lucky to have the enduring support of many people who've helped me immeasurably with this story, the books before, and—if I play my cards right—the tales to come. To my own fever of friends and family near and far: Thank you for listening and laughing. And as always, an extra spotlight on Marja, Megan, Boom, and Teach; thanks for the hours and hours (and hours and hours) talking this one out. Y'all are smart and funny and excellent. I'm ever so grateful to have you on my team.

Thank you to my editor, Orlando Dos Reis. Here we are at number six, and the opportunity to work on books together still feels like a dream come true. Thanks for your guidance and care with my characters every step of the way. A super-thanks to the Scholastic team behind the scenes, including Caroline Flanagan, Yaffa Jaskoll, Jessica White, Jackie Hornberger,

Lori Lewis, and Susan Hom that work their collective magic to make this book and every other whole.

To my swim consultants, Julia Rose (old swimmer's knee for life) and Nick Hernandez: Thank you for your invaluable insights into the world of middle school aquatics. For all things astrology, thank you, Cutie Silva. You're my favorite Pisces, and I can't wait to read your third memoir.

To my family—Mom, Dad, and Ham: Thank you always for everything, ever.

And to every reader out there: Thank you for using your imaginations to help bring Ellie's story and so many others to life.

About the Author

Jessie Paddock is the author of *Gemini Academy*, *The Crush Necklace*, *The Secrets Necklace*, *The Luck Necklace*, and *Swimming with Dolphins*. She holds an MFA in writing for children from the New School. She has lived in New York City for a while now, although she sometimes still misses her hometown of Atlanta. She loves summer, soccer, and riding her bike to places she's never been.